NIGHT SWEATS

TALES OF HOMOSEXUAL WONDER AND WOE

Visit us at www.boldstrokesbooks.com

NIGHT SWEATS

TALES OF HOMOSEXUAL WONDER AND WOE

by

Tom Cardamone

A Division of Bold Strokes Books

2016

NIGHT SWEATS: TALES OF HOMOSEXUAL WONDER AND WOE
© 2016 BY TOM CARDAMONE. ALL RIGHTS RESERVED.

ISBN 13: 978-1-62639-572-5

"OWL AERIE" PREVIOUSLY PUBLISHED AS "THE WEIGHT OF WISDOM," IN CHELSEA STATIONS #2, 2012
"THE CLOUD DRAGON ATE RED BALLOONS" ORIGINALLY PUBLISHED IN DAILY SCIENCE FICTION, 3/14/2011.
"ICE KING" PREVIOUSLY PUBLISHED IN UNMASKED II, STARBOOKS PRESS, 2009
A VERSION OF "MUTINOUS CHOCOLATE" PREVIOUSLY PUBLISHED IN BLACK FIRE, BOLD STROKES BOOKS, 2011
"OVERTIME AT THE BEHEADING FACTORY" PREVIOUSLY PUBLISHED IN SLICES OF FLESH, DARK MOON PRESS, 2012
"THE LOVE OF THE EMPEROR IS DIVINE" PREVIOUSLY PUBLISHED IN HANDSOME DEVIL, PRIME BOOKS 2014
"HONEYSUCKLE" PREVIOUSLY PUBLISHED IN GLITTERWOLF #3, 2013

THIS TRADE PAPERBACK ORIGINAL IS PUBLISHED BY
BOLD STROKES BOOKS, INC.
P.O. BOX 249
VALLEY FALLS, NY 12185

FIRST EDITION: JANUARY 2016

CREDITS
EDITOR: JERRY L. WHEELER
PRODUCTION DESIGN: STACIA SEAMAN
COVER ILLUSTRATION BY MEL ODOM
COVER DESIGN BY KATE SHANLEY

Acknowledgments

Special thanks to Len Barot, 'Nathan Burgoine, Cindy Cresap, Sandy Lowe, Stacia Seaman, Connie Ward, Jerry L. Wheeler, and all the folk at Bold Strokes Books for welcoming me into the fold.

To Leo

Finally, my story has a hero.

Tom

I write for beloved friends who can see colour in words, can smell the perfume in syllables in blossom, can be shocked with the fine elfish *electricity* of words.

—Lafcadio Hearn

Drops of Sweat

OWL AERIE

Our house was as gray and proper-looking as an ancient librarian, the shingled roof like papery fingers steepled in contemplation. High on a hill shrouded by spindly evergreens, the tall pines wept needles all year round, providing an endless opportunity to earn my allowance. Father would often join in on weekends, pipe clenched between his colorless lips as we raked the yard together, often dividing the expansive lawn into quadrants, gathering the pine needles and miscellaneous leaves into a chessboard of detritus. I particularly loved the autumn days when we burned the piles, smoke apocryphal, inviting misty thoughts of other worlds and ancient times. I'd throw pine cones into the fire and pretend they were black grenades about to explode a menacing gas that killed only adults. When we finished, my little sisters would bound out of the house in tights and tattered pink tutus, their frills mucked with peanut butter and jelly fingerprints. They giggled and tumbled across the yard as if the stage had been cleared for their spectacular performance.

The house itself was one of the oldest in town. Imposing in its prominence, it looked much larger on the outside than it felt on the inside. With gray boards, black shutters, and flaking shingles, the house was skeletal and ribbed with latticework wrapped by a porch that held on to the shadows no matter the time of day or the brightness of sun. Our paneled station wagon perfectly matched the somber, earthy colors of the house—it clung to the curlicue of the rocky driveway like a wistful Labrador banished from the garage, a black cavity so overstuffed with boxes of Christmas ornaments, forgotten tools, and unused camping and sporting equipment that we had no room for the weather-beaten car.

In the spring, Dad and I would clean out the gutters. He alone tended to the empty aerie above the attic. Removing twigs, smoking out the nascent hornet's nest, he'd go about the chore atop the longest ladder I'd ever seen as if it were just that, another chore, never hinting at the disappointment that surely tempered the joy he had achieved in establishing a handsome family, holding a steady job, and keeping a well-maintained yard.

When the Great Owls came to Gravesend, Massachusetts, they came silently and at night. Great Owls are unbelievably large, majestic, mythic creatures. You felt their presence subtly; the air tasted like it did after a major storm, refreshed from a chaos laid to rest. They brought with them a hunger for raccoons and stray cats and served as a source of munificent luck. If just the shadow of their considerable wingspan darkened your path, you were guaranteed to have a good year. At dusk, barren women lingered over laundry on the line, having known similarly challenged couples to have been blessed with twins after a Great Owl kept pace above their car for several yards on Beech Tree Road. Kids who got poor grades one year excelled the next if they found a feather on the playground. The size of tennis rackets, these silken treasures were coveted by the lucky families that possessed them, displayed under glass above mantels, placed beneath the bassinets of sick babies, passed down generation to generation. When one of these supernatural birds roosted in the aerie of a home for the summer, the privilege was most fortuitous.

All of the houses of Gravesend possessed discreet yet sizeable aeries, built like bell towers or peaks extended above the lay of the roof to invite nesting. As the majority of the homes were from the early nineteenth century, barely perceptible runic symbols believed to attract the owls were worked into the wood. But what brought them to Gravesend was worked into the soil, stitched into the fabric of our humble municipality. This was the particular magic of the whole of New Utrecht County, of which Gravesend was the county seat; the next hamlet down the road possessed one stoplight, a tiny A&P, and nearly luminescent tabbies that prolonged the life of their owners as long as they were sung to and oft petted. The water tower near Grays Farm attracted white deer with silver spots. If they eat from your hand, you will find true and everlasting love. They're skittish, though.

❖

The smell of Mom's freshly baked pecan pie wafted throughout the house and pulled us into the kitchen. Though it was early May, a chill lingered, tarnishing the additional sunlight granted by daylight saving time. Father forbade fires in the fireplace early spring. The pictures on the mantel above displayed our family in various stages of joy: Christmas, newborn, faded black-and-white photos of generations past. Mom left the oven door open while she worked in the kitchen, and the girls dutifully set the table. The house retained the cold, however. We usually wore sweaters indoors, so the heat pouring out of the oven was silently welcome.

Dad came to the table without a word, which signaled nothing more than tired contentment. As an accountant with his own storefront on Main Street, April was his busiest month; the spillover into May meant late nights and weekend work. With June came canoe trips and leisurely chatting with the neighbors over the shared and eternally peeling white picket fence. The girls colored on construction paper while I shredded the napkin in my lap. Mom had laid the evening paper beside Father's plate, along with a tumbler of rum and Coke. I could tell from the drink's caramel gravity that she'd made it a strong one, had probably thought of dispensing with the newspaper altogether, but decided its absence was more conspicuous than the contents.

Listed proudly alongside the obituaries, those families that had landed a Great Owl had their names in print. An august notice, Byzantine font, and the symbol of an owl in flight, the same image the paper had used since its inception in 1899. I longed for the evening comics page; Urchin Andy had been cornered by the Chimney Creep, and though I was desperate to find out if and how he had escaped the culprit's sooty clutches, asking for the section would call attention to the newspaper, circle, in bright, flaky yellow crayon the esteemed names of the families benefiting from owls in their aeries, underscoring the fact that our house had gone unvisited ever since the year I was born.

❖

School let out, and summer spread its picnic blanket over the town and unpacked typical delights: drifting fireflies at twilight, raw, humid mornings that gathered force into afternoon thunderstorms, cloudless days where the heat melted the hours, and I drained Slurpees from 7-Eleven and counted coins so I could purchase another packet of Topps Baseball cards. The town was abuzz with gossip on two fronts: a Great

Barn Owl had ensconced itself in the garage of a family in the Greendale subdivision, displacing their Range Rover and marking the first time an owl had strayed from one of the original homesteads of Gravesend. The family, new to town and busy with an infant, was perplexed and proud. They talked about their esteemed guest to everyone every chance they got, in the supermarket parking lot, while in line at the dry cleaners, seeking advice from neighbors who were in turn shocked by their phenomenal luck as well as the impropriety of their statements. This was something people just did not discuss in public. By now the list of homes who had received an owl was nearly complete, and the town typically turned its attention to civic matters and Little League, excepting that the Symonses' owl had yet to roost.

The Symons were one of the oldest families in Gravesend, and the wealthiest in New Utrecht. They'd given the town several mayors and yearly donated the funds to pay for the Fourth of July fireworks. Mr. Symons had his taxes done in Boston and was thus not Father's client. I knew his daughters distantly. Though only a few years older, they seemed like miniature, blessed adults; they moved through the halls of high school in a somewhat equestrian manner, as if they were always practicing for greater things. The family name had yet to appear in the paper alongside the requisite inky avian imprint.

Word was that the senior Symons demanded the paper run the family name in anticipation of the event, but his order had fallen on deaf ears—literally. The ancient editor, Franklin Sacks, had long claimed his hearing had been damaged as a boy by an unusually low burst of fireworks one Fourth of July and had held a grudge against the Symonses ever since. All of which Mother dutifully reported to Father at the dinner table, working hard to maintain a neutral tone and suppress the glee she naturally felt, for Mrs. Symons was head of the local Rotary Club and had blocked Mom's more liberal charity initiatives at every turn.

At their last meeting in the library's small auditorium, Mrs. Symons announced with much forced cheer that Mr. Symons had surprised the family with a grand tour of Europe. They would be leaving in a fortnight and traveling the continent for two months, and she would necessarily relinquish the Rotary presidency for the duration of the trip. Mom was thrilled and thought her absence an opportunity to refresh membership—a reference to the Greendale wife blessed by a Great Barn Owl. I didn't add that one of the Bellamy brothers, on his morning paper route a few weeks ago, saw Mr. Symons arguing vigorously with the witch who lives at the end of Beech Tree Road. I had seen her too, once, riding her rickety bike past our house early one morning, its basket stuffed with emerald toads to be pressed into potions, the witch's gray hair wild and thick, like straw on a blown-out broom.

Father took such gossip in stride. His only comment, while absently slicing and serving up another helping of roast beef to all around, was that he hoped the sudden absence of the Symonses didn't affect the Fourth of July festivities, which sent a hush across the dining room table. He smiled to himself, having reasserted his authority with ease, but the lines at the corner of his eyes looked deeper, their inlay established by weariness instead of wisdom.

❖

I rode my bike to the baseball game along with some of the other guys on the team, weaving in and out of each other's paths, laughing, waving to neighbors we knew, seeing who could pop a wheelie, ride the longest with their hands behind their back. I was terrible at bat but a great outfielder; I could catch any ball and turn it around to the nearest base in a split second but was still a nervous pitcher. Our summer uniforms were perpetually grass-stained and smelled of the game: churned clay and earnest sweat. I wove my bike around a yawning pothole and wondered if Ken from drama class would be in the stands.

He always wore the same black shirt, tight not for fashion's sake but because he'd recently outgrown it. I liked how it rode up on his arms and receded from his widening alabaster neck. Crisp blond hair lay lightly like snow on his shoulders, in contrast to the darkness of his questioning eyebrows. Last semester the crossed wits of our in-class discussion had easily carried on into the hall, demanding extension, elucidation. We'd naturally suggested, practically at the same time, meeting up later to chat about the play in question, breathlessly laughing over the choice of the female lead, only to falter. Haltingly Ken offered an excuse, hand heavy on my shoulder, eyes penetrating yet still murky. In the cadence of his withdrawal was the unfocused fear that my offer to come over to my house invited something deeper than friendship. Yet all I wanted, all I needed, all I could handle in the fragile porcelain of my youth, was that and only that.

In the last inning, little Jimmy Farragut was at bat. He always hit a grounder, so I was lost in thought. Thirsty and tired, I debated putting my bike in the back of the station wagon and hitching a ride with my family or riding home with the guys and eating at McDonald's, though the usual cashier was a former jock from school who chided us if we lost a game. The stands went quiet, so I squinted at home plate and saw Jimmy's bat go limp as he looked up, hand shielding his eyes. I panicked, thinking Jimmy had finally knocked one out of the park, and started to run backward, mitt out, as a vast black shadow swallowed my body. The darkness cooled the sweat on my brow and calmed my heart. Though the shadow of the enormous owl swiftly passed, it felt like time had stopped. I could read stars and celestial pathways within the dark richness that its wingspan projected onto the surrounding grass. Opening my mouth in awe, a refreshing chill poured down my throat, a tonic of shade and magic. And then the Great Owl was gone. I could feel the ends of its feathers comb my flesh as the sun hit my eyes. Instinct took over, and I effortlessly caught the round object dropped from its talons.

Hooking my fingers around it, I nearly tossed it to home plate when I realized it was bigger than a baseball. A human skull stared vacantly up at me out of my battered glove.

❖

Dad argued vigorously and respectfully with the police officers behind the bleachers. From their stances, I could tell he was not only making a strong argument, but he was winning. We weren't allowed to take the jawless skull home, much to Mom's relief, though Father had been able to get a guarantee it would be returned once the police investigation was completed. This mysterious event was unprecedented, perplexing, and brought a large amount of attention to our household. That night a neighbor returned a leaf blower he'd borrowed months ago as an excuse to linger on the porch. Cars slowed as they drove by, and the phone rang off the hook. The next day's evening newspaper, unsure of how to handle such a unique episode in the town's history while maintaining its usual discretion, printed our family name in the space reserved for those with an owl in residence, though with a unique flourish. The image of an owl in flight was printed in gold instead of black. Mother had proudly left the newspaper beside Dad's plate. We exchanged knowing looks as he casually made his way to said section, and we were surprised when, after pausing at the page with our name in print, he pushed back his chair and left the room without a word. The girls were startled—one of them dropped her fork on the floor. Mom rushed to soothe her as we heard the car start outside. Silent confusion reigned at the dinner table as Mom muttered something about Dad probably needing tobacco for his pipe, though she kept her back to us and fussed over the cherry pie in the oven, lest we read the concern so obvious in her voice, on her face as well.

I was frozen in my seat. *Did I embarrass him? What if he doesn't come back?* Just as these dark, cloudy thoughts were in danger of churning into an internal storm of doubt, the station wagon pulled up in the drive. Mom could no longer contain herself and rushed to meet him. The girls tumbled after her as if pulled by invisible strings while I remained firmly rooted in my seat, preparing for whatever punishment or pronouncement was to come. Mom's laughter, one part surprise, two parts relief, announced that the matter was one of joy, and as I let out a huge sigh, Father marched into the room with a stack of evening papers in hand.

"I bought every single last one at the gas station. They wouldn't have any left by the morning, and when my son makes history in this town, you better believe we're going to celebrate it!"

The girls did a little dance around his legs as Mom gingerly relieved him of the stack of papers. They exchanged a look in the process that was a mixture of pride and something else, a flicker of light, a shared ember that made me jealous and curious. Flustered, I thought of Ken but quickly banished the image from my mind, relishing that he would again resurface no matter what. We poured onto the porch, and Mom followed us with a pitcher of lemonade. Fireflies alighted on the grass as the sky bruised, and the strongest stars pushed through the veil of dusk. The girls cartwheeled across the lawn, and a neighbor walking his dog crossed the street just so he could say hello. Dad gave him a silent salute, finally the admiral of his own ship. At first I thought his ride to the gas station provided a moment alone, a chance for him to decide that indeed the skull was a sign of fortune, and as the town's opinion of the event had coalesced, culminating with the gold owl in the newspaper, so too did he need to come to terms with it. And with me.

Mother stood behind my rocking chair and absently played with my hair, something she hadn't done since I was small. Later that night, after I mounted the stairs and went to my room, the brand new catcher's mitt on my bed signaled to me that Dad had known all along.

Downstairs a canned laugh track leapt from the television in timed intervals like a wizened jack-in-the-box. My parents chortled on cue. I finished sorting my baseball cards for doubles to trade, pulled the tiny gold chain cord beneath the emerald hood of the brass banker's lamp that graced the nicked art deco rolltop desk, and sat patiently in my pajamas. After my bath, my flesh felt kneaded and raw. The television downstairs hushed. The stairs creaked. I remained still, a thin stork perched on the shoal of the night, fishing the silence for opportunity. Calm encased the house like gift wrap. With practiced stealth, I rose quietly from the normally squeaky chair. I made my way deftly down the hall past framed and faded cameos of forgotten family members, barely touching the carpet, reaching the stairs to the attic in complete darkness. I'd left its door slightly ajar earlier in the evening. The cool brass knob felt like a small moon in my hot hands. I was sweating, and as I took the stairs up to the attic, the pajamas stuck to my back. I imagined the material made transparent as sweat spotted my backside; my pajama bottoms bunched at my rear like cloth pulled into oiled gears.

The door to the attic proper stuck and, for a moment, my heart stopped as well but then it gave and opened upon the boxed and labeled contents of our family's past: broken bassinets and clothing and stacks of *National Geographic* magazine, their gold borders washed white by the moonlight streaming into the room through the large octagonal window that marked the center of the roof's peak. I made my way quietly to the large oval mirror atilt on its antique stand and caught sight of my image turned a ghostly white: dark hair wild, plastered to my forehead and shooting out in the back. The cords of my neck worked vigorously. My whole body was a well of alternating buckets filled with either fear or exhilaration.

Exhilaration won out as, facing my full reflection, I slowly unbuttoned my pajama top. Bare-chested, I examined the nautical lines of my ribs, the open book of my chest, the pages blank, as yet unsullied by hair or the touch of another boy. I lifted my arms, sniffed each hollow and smelled faint sour milk, and was disappointed that my body had yet to produce the musk of a man. The hair there was slight and dormant. I thought of each pit as holding the curl of a hibernating animal, half-formed and sluggish. No amount of pull-ups and yard work had yet to excite the growl of an appropriate stench. I touched a pale nipple. and it rose instantly while its mate lay dormant. All of which conjured a tightness in my pajama bottoms. In a practiced step I pulled them down to my knees with the heels of each foot tugging on the sag of both cuffs. My reflection in the mirror sharpened—a wavering quarter moon ready for exploration.

❖

People all over town wanted a piece of my luck. When I grabbed lunch with friends at McDonald's, the know-it-all behind the counter slid me a free milkshake. After two weeks, I made sure I rode my bike everywhere I went because if I walked down the sidewalk, countless people would offer me a ride in their car. Dad had been contacted by a large company looking to expand into New Utrecht County and had been hired as a consultant at a rate that, he breathlessly announced, "would change everything." Mom's desire to bring fresh blood to the Rotary Club had met with success, and she was further rewarded by being asked, in Mrs. Symons's absence, to chair the group that selected new charity initiatives.

On the way to baseball practice, I stopped by Billowing Cape Comics and Collectibles. I'd quit buying comic books two years ago after I started checking out books from the library and playing sports, but I still kept up with a few titles. The owner nodded as I came in. He had a reputation for being snotty to his younger clientele, though he was always nice to me. Only in his late twenties, he watched kids closely for shoplifting and limited the number of titles he would put on hold for anyone under sixteen. More kids crowded into the store. Kids I didn't really know said "Hi" and patted me on the back. I heard my name whispered but was already growing weary of this newfound attention. The owner of the shop beckoned me over and handed me a brown paper bag.

He fingered his uneven goatee. "Here's a few promo copies of some new titles you might like."

The nearest kids stared at this unusual act of generosity. I was dumbfounded—my cheeks went flushed. We used to talk for hours about the complex mythologies of certain superheroes and declaim movie adaptations that were obviously unfaithful to a character's origins and abilities. But now this friendliness seemed overt, with unfocused expectations attached. I nearly dropped the paper bag while stammering, "Thanks."

The owner sensed the gift was too revealing and offered a practiced shrug.

"These are titles I don't collect. I just wanted to give them to *anybody* rather than throw them out."

It came too late; the energy in the room had changed—as if a song had finished and somehow the silence before the next was louder than any music. With that, the front door opened, and the bell above it jangled. The boys who tumbled in filled the store with raucous laughter, and the owner gratefully turned his attention to a small child over-laden with boxes of colorful figurines, a bored mother prodding him toward the counter. I hastened toward the door and promptly bumped into Ken. He'd seen me coming but didn't get out of the way. He gave me a big, sincere smile and shot a soft punch into my shoulder as I passed.

"Nice catch."

I returned his smile and peeled out of the store. It was only later, looking over the new comics spread across my bed, the comic store owner's phone number scrawled lightly on a discarded receipt, that I wondered what he really meant.

❖

August brought mosquitoes, trips to the pool at the tennis club, and the police to our door with a brown cardboard file box containing the skull. They'd called and arranged a time to drop it off, joking that they'd considered just putting it in the mailbox but worried the postman might find it first. Dad asked a few perfunctory questions, but everyone understood some things happened in New Utrecht that didn't necessarily have to make sense. The police's main concern was the skull might have been dropped by a Great Burrowing Owl and thought it necessary to check the local cemeteries to see if any graves had been disturbed.

After the police left, mother exhaled with a deep resignation that she'd cleared a spot in the attic for the box. Earlier, I had heard her and Dad talking in the backyard, behind laundry lines hoisting waves of linen and twisting tutus. She didn't want the "thing," as she called it, in the house. She thought, at best, that it should be buried in the backyard. Father was more circumspect. Smoke from his pipe unwound over floral sheets.

"Yes, dear, I see, I see. But at the end of the day, it belongs to the boy."

So I was given the following weeks to decide what to do with the skull. But the owls have never dropped anything except the occasional giant feather into the lives of Gravesend residents, so I was at a complete loss. I tried to remember Newton's Laws of Gravity that we had studied in science class but couldn't imagine that even in a vacuum a giant feather would have the same velocity as a human skull. And now the skull was in the house, Mother sounded distraught, as if its presence would add negative ballast to her dreams. I peered into the box. It rested on a folded blanket like a napping kitten. The nose hole was an ancient and complex cavern; the cranium a sturdy egg. As my parents busied themselves in the kitchen, I hoisted the box under one arm and went outside, letting the screen door slam shut to broadcast my departure.

❖

The heaviness of the box kept it grounded in my lap as I aimed my bike toward the New Utrecht County Library on Main

Street. The library was an old building, similar in design to the courthouse it faced on the opposite side of the town square. I visited regularly under the pretext of doing homework without the interruption of my sisters and the pull of the television. But really, I first came here to learn about myself. I checked out the typical fantasy and science fiction novels, but in the nonfiction stacks, when I was sure no one else was around, I studiously pored over medical and psychology books about "homosexuality." The information was scary, exhilarating, yet scientific, matter-of-fact and cold. As often as not, I would retreat to the men's room in the library basement. In the stalls, fresh paint barely concealed words and drawings crude and alluring, hinting at more primal knowledge than the books offered. So far I had yet to encounter anything that explained the shudder I experienced in the moonlit attic or the ecstasy of sliding into home plate, cutting across the lanky shadows of my teammates painted by the afternoon sun across the red dirt, wishing Ken were in the bleachers, cheering me on.

The librarian smiled quizzically as I hefted the box up onto the counter. The old woman retained a healthy hue from weekend gardening that had, conversely, warped her posture as much as the books she pored over. Her glasses were huge ovals perched on a tiny, beakish nose. She gave a serene, expectant nod after surveying the contents of the box and beckoned for me to follow. Between the dusty marble pillars topped with intricate owl carvings in the foyer was a tall glass cabinet of historical items: trophies of high school sports victories long forgotten, faded photographs, arrowheads, and assorted curios. She sorted the appropriate key from among many on a large loop that hung around her neck from a string so frayed it blended with her white hair. She unlocked the cabinet, and together we studied the contents. With a contemplative finger on her lips, she knelt and shifted a worn cricket bat on the bottom shelf, gifted to Gravesend by a visiting Royal a decade ago, and patted the area as if inviting a pet to hop up on her lap. I solemnly placed the skull inside. She locked the cabinet, and we admired the skull which, in turn, looked unblinkingly through us. I liked that it wasn't centrally placed, that it was now a cornerstone in the haphazard town history collected within the cabinet. She rested her ancient hand lightly on my shoulder for a moment, and then returned to the desk where a patron patiently waited to check out a stack of books.

I sped home, lest my parents grow anxious. The entire family was waiting for me in the kitchen, the makings for sandwiches spread across the table: an open jar of mayonnaise with a knife sticking out of it, a loaf of expertly sliced bread fanned out like a deck of cards on the cutting board, sticky sheets of ham in a bunch, nearly luminescent pickles slid around a butter dish.

Before I could eat or tell my family what I had done with our accidental, providential heirloom, one act remained. Taking the stairs two at a time, sweaty, determined, I burst into my bedroom and stole my old glove from atop the broken skateboard in the back of the closet. I headed back downstairs. Laughter from the girls flittered throughout the house as a shift in the clouds sent rays of golden sunshine into the living room. Above the fireplace, I separated the framed photographs in the center of the mantel and placed it there, palm out, reaching for the sky.

MS FOUND IN A BOOKSTORE

Certain patrons of Metzengerstein Magazines and Books know about the attic and its alluring contents, but none know of the basement and its extensive subterranean treasure. The old man who runs Metzengerstein's hired me only because he couldn't get rid of me. I'd been moping around the store daily all through high school. Then whenever I wasn't in any of my community college classes, I was there reading comics and coveting dog-eared paperbacks. I never bought anything, and he figured that given a pittance of a salary, I'd finally return some coin to the register. He was right. His failing eyesight and a growing disinterest in small talk or anything generally related to customers put me behind the counter while he shuffled about. When I wasn't restocking magazines and shooing kids away from the comic book rack, I swept the sloping, uneven aisles and stacked and restacked books to keep the inevitable avalanches at bay, hiding coveted titles until payday.

Occasionally, always a weekday, always before we opened, and almost always in the summer, the old man would order me to meet a customer at the bookstore well before we opened and accompany them upstairs into the attic. I was instructed to be present but invisible, to assist in any way possible while resolutely leaving them alone. Though the attic was a world unto itself, a place without order or rules, I was no angelic gatekeeper, but as lost and as mystified as the customers. Here time stopped and treasure floated to the surface among a sea of books, boxes of books, rickety gray splintered shelves poured forth a waterfall of volumes, manuscripts, letters—and the customers, mouths agape, not knowing what to do with their hands so fingers hung in the air, vibrating like humming bird wings until they could gather the courage to alight on the flower that blossomed within their heart: the hand-scrawled manuscript of the last book of an incomplete trilogy, the author dead of cirrhosis. The coveted children's book, title long forgotten, opened to the very page that set their dreams afire. Signed editions long sought, privately published ancestral memoirs, always what the customer was looking for. *Always*.

And I was dumbfounded. Jealous of their joy, hungry for the satisfaction that welled in their eyes, I marveled at how subtly the attic curved to their desires. For the divorceé who reclaimed a certain art book, the attic ceiling bent with the promise of a tree house and seemed to fill with buttery, Turneresque light. One elderly gentlemen scoured the boxes and shelves for a collection of short stories, the sole book of an author rumored to have committed suicide on the day of publication—hoping a bit of notoriety would boost sales, only to have them all remaindered. On that August morning, I had broken a sweat waiting for him at the entrance of the bookstore, but in the attic a pervading chill wove its way through the room. I kept clutching at my neck. Every shadow seemed to crawl toward me, and as the stooped patron let out an audible gasp of delight, only then did I recall the author in question had hanged himself.

I never knew how these collectors and seekers made arrangements to peruse the attic, only that the price was agreed upon before entry and paid without hesitation once the book they sought was in their hands. Yet I didn't have a title of my own that was so out of reach, so valuable as to be consigned as a missing part of my spirit. I always found the books I wanted, the tattered comics I craved at yard sales and Metzengerstein's itself.

One particular customer set me reeling, one of the summer people that flood our town seasonally, buying and selling summer homes with the same ease locals purchased groceries. Their beautiful children galloped through the town square, their laughter a summer song that announced to shopkeepers it was time to elevate their prices. He always bought hardbacks. First editions, serious American literature one summer, biographies the next, fantastically linked: F. Scott Fitzgerald, Hemingway, then a book detailing their rivalrous friendship in Paris, then another title about the construction of the Eiffel Tower, then everything by or about Cocteau, books like pearls on a necklace. Each purchase made me more curious.

He was one of those rare summer people who came in the autumn and visited while spring was still misty, with a chill that lasted until late into the day. Older, his hair still blond and boyish, the lines on his face were stenciled by curiosity, not worry. He wore his wealth casually, worn chinos early June, relaxing into J. Crew shorts as the town heated up, with oxford shirts always open at the collar. Once, as I was handing him his change, I couldn't take my eyes off the golden hair that circled his tanned wrist. He thought I was admiring his Rolex and smiled. "It was a gift. I think they're a bit ostentatious, but…" I grinned and I know I blushed. That unfinished sentence stretched for miles, grew into a thick and thorny fence that separated us. We lived in different worlds. I had nothing to offer him. The old man had caught the exchange between us and cackled, "Never bet the devil your head."

He roared until he coughed, fished out the dirty spoon he

kept in his distended shirt pocket, and poured himself a dollop of plum-colored cough medicine from one of the many dusty half-empty bottles omnipresent throughout the shop.

The old man napped behind the register on slow days, leaving me to read among the stacks. After we'd had several sales from the attic, he would go down into the basement and shuffle around. I'd hear muffled swearing through the door and the sound of boxes being kicked. Then silence. He'd be gone long enough for me to worry. Just as I was about to call out his name, I'd hear him struggle to pull or push a box up the stairs. He'd practically collapse as the door swung shut behind him. Several times I offered to retrieve the boxes myself, but he always ignored me. It was one of the few rules he was strict about. I was to never go down into the basement.

❖

The tinkling gooey glitter of familiar disco dripped from the speakers mounted above the bar. I sipped my weak Jack and Coke and listened as Gladys told another funny story about mishaps with summer people at the diner where she waited tables. I chewed my straw as she checked her phone yet again to see if the cute boy from our English class had called or texted her yet. We were best friends in high school and now took the same courses at the community college to get our grades up so we could eventually go to State. She was in a rush to get into a drama program, and I let her ambitions pull me along. I was happy working at Metzengerstein's, but knew I needed an excuse to leave town. My life needed more momentum than reading obscure science fiction and fantasy novels, getting lost in comic books, and thinking about men but never touching them. We hung out at the Purloined Bottle most weekend nights. It was the town's only gay bar. I knew all of the other regulars by sight: the local lesbian couple with whom we often joked and played darts, the prim gay summer people who always sat in the same booths. One of my professors and I studiously ignored each other every Friday. He always went home with a boy who looked just like me.

The bartender, Ambrose, knew we were a year shy of drinking age and liked to tease me and Gladys before serving us. He was the most flamboyant character in town. He had aged past his looping pirate earrings but wouldn't be recognizable without them. His bad highlights and Hawaiian shirts stretched to the limit by an expansive beer belly would have been farcical if he hadn't been in on the joke. The handwritten sign above the bar stated *No Attitude, No Cussing, and We Fucking Mean It*. Winking at every customer, reflective Mardi Gras beads swirling around his neck, he kept the liquor flowing. As I grabbed a bar stool, he shouted the same old joke, "How's your sex life, junior?"

"So far it's pretty theoretical, Ambrose." He howled and poured us our usual. I was about to challenge Gladys to a game of darts when she nodded toward the door.

"Look, that's him, the big tipper."

I turned without a care. The Purloined Bottle is so small it's impossible to be discreet, or as I once heard Ambrose say over the phone while giving directions, "We're right after the A&P, but if you don't turn before you see the sign, you'll miss us. We're a size four, honey."

I'd heard about the big tipper for years. He always left a ten for lunch and a twenty for dinner, regardless of the bill. All the waitresses kissed up to him, but he had a preference for Gladys, and every summer she remembered that he liked his tea sweet. It was him. My blond book buyer, the King of the Summer People. He sidled up to the bar next to us and Ambrose poured him a whiskey, neat, without asking. *If he's a regular, too, how come I've never seen him here?* I turned to Gladys, but she had slid from her bar stool and was pulling darts out of the pocked dart board. I ambled up to her with a questioning look. She tucked her chin into her neck like she always does when she wants to whisper.

"I'm just *really* surprised to see him here. After all, he has a family. Wife and kids." She straightened her back, took aim, and let a dart fly. It hit its target as a lump rose within my throat.

❖

The next day he came in and lingered in the travel section, *The Wall Street Journal* folded under one arm. I tried to keep him out of my line of sight and dusted the poetry section at the other end of the shop. His literary taste had occasionally hinted he was gay, but he'd always come into the store alone, so the double surprise of seeing him at the Purloined Bottle and finding out he was married left me numb. When Gladys learned he was my crush from the bookstore, she questioned me relentlessly and for all the wrong reasons. Townsfolk loved to gossip about summer people, what their purchases revealed about their personalities, how they overuse our first names—which they thought was folksy but somehow implied a sense of ownership to us. The men in town who looked after their properties during the harsh winters, checking on pipes, repairing roofs, reported to their wives which families had a television in *every* room, which married men ordered firewood so they could bring other women up on snowy weekends. But I didn't want to talk about my summer man. Gladys had had two beers and was blind to my reticence, so I reminded her the twenty dollar tips were in jeopardy if word got out, and then I changed the topic. The Pixies were playing in the city next month, and we needed to not only get tickets, but ensure her olive green Dodge Dart, with liver spots of rust and a bent antenna, was up to the journey.

The old man was conspicuously absent from the register when the summer man wanted to be rung up. He purchased two books on Budapest, and I recalled a string of Robert Graves's first editions he had purchased the year before, and then coffee table books on Constantinople, the poetic fireworks of July turned into August architecture. I dropped coins into the overturned cupola of his hand and bravely searched his eyes for recognition from last night and he smiled back as always, open and carefree. As he left, the bell above the door rung with a silvery sound. The old man coughed distantly from the basement, and I went over to the travel section to fill the dark slices of shadow that he'd left among the titles.

❖

Gladys's Dodge Dart sputtered and died a week before the concert. She sold her ticket to help pay for the repairs and I feigned disappointment, grumbled about going to the concert by myself, but I relished some time alone in the city. I took the bus in early and haunted my favorite bookstores, hoping to gather up enough courage to go to a gay bar before the show. I'd been with Gladys before. The bars were endless caverns, the music preposterously loud, and the bartenders all shirtless, the spikes of their nipples so sharp they could cut glass. I wasn't into the opening band and relished the idea that I might actually meet someone, kiss a guy my own age for once, and have an excuse to miss the midnight bus back home. I had a few hours before the show, so I ate a cheap meal in Chinatown, then scoured several places for books. I'd recently graduated from Piers Anthony to books of cloaked desire, and peeked at copies of *Querelle* before scooping up a battered paperback of *Maldoror*. After being rung up, I started to tuck the book into my backpack, and as I turned, the blond customer appeared in the doorway. He unfurled a wry smile.

"You're not cheating on Mr. Metzengerstein, are you?"

I gave him a puzzled look and then laughed. Many people confuse the old man as being the namesake for the store, but he claims he bought the business decades ago and simply kept the name so he wouldn't have to pay for new signage. The summer man was dressed in a suit but with a flowing tan overcoat that made him look relaxed and in command at the same time. A man used to warm climes and cocktails. I tried to squeeze by him, but he put a finger on my shoulder and looked at the title in my hand. He locked his gaze on the surreal cover art of my pitiable copy and for just a moment I thought he was going to snatch it away from me. I would have gladly let him have it and more, but then he nodded.

"Right, I have an edition from the twenties with illustrations by Odilon Redon."

He moved past me, but I didn't want to let the moment go.

"Next time you're in the store, if the old man isn't around, I'll take you up to the attic. I bet we have whatever you're looking for there."

I couldn't believe what I had said, but he turned to me and mouthed a silent "thank you," tipping his head in a curious way that somehow indicated he had been waiting for an invitation long overdue.

I danced like I never danced before. I rode every wave of mutilation the band laid out as if I were surfing in the midnight. Sweat dripped off my chin, and when a boy looked at me too long, I walked up to him and put my hands on his hips. We swayed for a moment together, eyes locked, before the crowd parted us. I left mid-song so I could make it to the bus station in time, not because I was worried that I would miss my bus, but because I wanted to be on time for work the next day. Because the summer man would be waiting for me.

❖

The bell above the front door rang just as the old man stepped into the basement. I looked up and saw the summer man. We smiled together as if on a date. He wore white tennis shorts, and the collar of his shirt was half up, as if he'd just come from playing touch football with some spare Kennedys. He seemed out of breath, excited, and he goaded me on with raised eyebrows. I enjoyed our conspiracy of silence and walked swiftly through the stacks, beckoning him to follow. He kept close. I felt his hot breath on my neck. When the floorboards groaned beneath our combined weight, we stifled giggles as I unlocked the door to the attic. The staircase was loaded with boxes of old *LIFE* magazines. The sconces on the wall bloomed as I flipped the switch. We took the stairs two at a time, and I opened the door to the attic with a butler's flourish. He ignored my bow and entered the room.

I watched as he rummaged through the boxes and ran a finger across the shelves. Every time I had been to the attic with a customer, it had felt different. This time, the room felt as it must feel when it's unoccupied. The light was flat. The books looked like the books you'd find at a Salvation Army. I felt he was browsing only to satisfy me, and none of the tomes he briskly handled interested him. Dejected, suddenly worried that the old man would find out and fire me, I felt the urge to rush back downstairs. I cleared my throat.

"What are you looking for?"

He looked at me, and as he answered the attic contracted to a dark and hot spot and the books opened to breathe humid fumes of lust and disenchantment.

"I'm not looking for anything in particular."

The attic snapped back into a dusty interior, and he was less than an inch from my face. His breath smelled of dank cinnamon.

"But what do you expect from a small-town bookstore?" He shrugged, and I burned with the contempt everyone here felt when the procession of summer people rolled through *our* town. They knew we couldn't live without their money, and they broadcast it constantly in little ways. Yet with his back to me, as he descended the stairs, I couldn't help myself.

"Come back at closing time, and I'll show you the basement."

Darkness silently swallowed his head.

❖

At closing time, I counted the till and glanced more than once at the door. We hadn't had a customer for over an hour, rare for that time of year. Main Street looked as if it had been cleared for a parade that never came. The old man had grumbled about closing early, and I thought that he somehow knew I had offered to show the customer the basement, that he was toying with me—that as we locked the door, he would hold his hand out for my keys in silent dismissal.

The summer man never came. I stuffed the money into the safe, and the old man left me at the curb without so much as a good-bye. I called Gladys from the payphone at the A&P and told her to meet me at the Purloined Bottle.

"Like we have anywhere else to go," she replied. "I'm

working a double and will meet you there later." She hung up, and I sauntered toward the bar, my backpack still heavy with the books I'd bought in the city. In my excitement to get back to the bookstore, I'd forgotten to take them out. Now they weighed on me like a thousand years of regret.

I'd never been to the bar so early, and Ambrose perked up as I walked in. He sensed I was in a bad mood, however, and poured me a stiff one. And then another. The local lesbians were there, coaxing me back outside. We shared a joint in their ancient VW van plastered with every liberal bumper sticker ever manufactured. They explained how their weed was home grown and after we were pretty high, they asked me too many questions about Gladys. I answered generously, expounding on aspects of her sex life which I knew nothing about, until we all laughed and poured out of the van and back into the bar.

The Purloined Bottle was now unusually packed, and everyone felt like dancing. Gladys made it. We did shots together, and I explained the local lesbians were planning on kidnapping her and dressing her in overalls to make her a slave in their pot garden. They overheard and threatened to feed me to their famously voluptuous cats, Virginia and Muddy. I ordered another drink and danced like I did at the Pixies concert, liberated and libidinous, reaching for the boy I had surreptitiously been staring at for the last few months. Instead, my hand landed on the shoulders of my summer man. He laughed, surprised, and put his hand on my waist and moved with me, winking at Gladys, shouting over the music for Ambrose to serve everyone a round of drinks on him. Applause, and we all did shots, and his hand never left my waist, it weighed on me like a heavy belt. Gladys gave me the eye. I wanted to ask her to stay with us but couldn't think of a way to say it. She took my silence as a dismissal, but as she slunk away, the summer man grabbed her, and the three of us danced. The bar grew smaller, more intimate than ever before, and a daring attitude raced through the room. The local lesbians took off their shirts and danced in their bras. A gay couple, summer people who always drank quietly alone, cornered a college student and made out with him, their omnipresent collie nosing their clashing knees with a perpetual whine. More shots and Ambrose jumped up on the bar and sang along to Dolly Parton's "Jolene" on the jukebox and everyone howled and more shots were poured. The summer man whispered cinnamon secrets in my ear while tugging on the belt loop of my jeans. And I told him everything, dreams I never shared, truths I had discovered, desires I had yet to act on.

I don't remember leaving the Purloined Bottle, only how our laughter scattered across the asphalt like broken glass as we stumbled among the few cars still parked on Main Street. I had fished the store keys out of my pocket and inserted them into the lock before I knew we were back at Metzengerstein's. He withdrew his hands from around my waist and squared his shoulders as I opened the door. I stumbled over the threshold as he slipped in behind me and I collapsed, laughing on the floor, as he quietly closed and locked the door behind us. Without a word, he crossed the room, stepped behind the register, and opened the door to the basement. I struggled to my feet, breathless, hands out. I shouted meekly, "Wait." But he slipped into the darkness and was gone.

I hesitated. The basement opening was a black gate. I looked out the window at the street lights, the parked cars, a starless night sky. The window scene was like a cheap painting, a billboard for a banal world without promise, just desperate repetition. The oblong rectangle of the basement door was a deliciously deep ocean filled with unknown things. I dove in.

❖

My eyes adjusted to the darkness as I tried to catch up to the summer man. I could see him up ahead, past teetering stacks of books, bending over a chest. The basement was vast. Its floor was earthen, like an ancient root cellar, and spread in every direction under the street and below other buildings, much farther than the scope of the bookstore. Books and sheaves of paper lay everywhere. I looked over my summer man's shoulder and saw he was giddily dipping into a chest filled with pulpy paperbacks. The covers were all plain: *The Fellow Traveler* series, erotic writings from the '60s, and beneath these titles, yellowed and typed manuscripts, stories submitted to the publisher but too lurid to print.

Gleeful with discovery, he chortled and held up these waylaid treasures, but I tried to shush him as the old man approached. I was shocked he would be in the basement at this hour, sure he would scold us and that my job had just been lost, but I noticed subtle differences as he approached. *This* old man was shirtless, wearing a worn leather apron and dusty work boots. His mouth hung open like an exhausted catfish. As he came closer, I could discern his eyes were covered by a white smear of viscous cataracts. A similar old man labored up ahead, putting books into a crate. I moved past my summer man and stumbled over a stack of books.

"Careful!" he snapped and gathered up the books I'd knocked over. I helped him: they were titles I'd never heard of from the Olympia Press. Books on torture, translations of ancient erotica, memoirs of historical figures I was only dimly aware of. The summer man moved feverishly, sweat curling his blond hair like flame, desperate to have all of these titles. But as he filled his arms with forgotten lore, another stack caught his eye, and he would gingerly set his prized possessions aside to collect more.

I followed him through a maze of books. Old men labored silently around us. All equally blind, each in turn completely ignored us. We turned a corner and found a twisting stairwell carved into black rock. Without hesitation, he descended and I followed, my mouth dry, sweat stains encircling my armpits. Below, more old men worked ancient shelves of books as if in a coal mine. The patron let out a whimper of joy at the first volume he lifted from the shelves. The ancient book was larger than usual with pages waxy and thick. I couldn't make out the script. He sensed my confusion and kissed me. His tongue was cold, metallic. I yearned for him to give me more, to drop the book and put his hands on me, but when we disengaged, I could read the Latin text. The lost writings of Tacitus. The next volume on the shelf was a biography of infamous whores by Procopius. I saw poetry from Petronius and plays by the Emperor Nero. The summer man was rapturous. We took turns reading forgotten words out loud to each other and took inspiration from these wicked texts. His arctic mouth devoured parts of me I had never surrendered before and when I hesitantly felt for him, I was not surprised that he was hot to the touch. When I grasped the part of him I needed most, I found coarse fur and serpentine strength. He never took his eyes off the page.

❖

And so we moved through the underground warren. A nest of pages swirled around us, unbound manuscripts came apart, unfurled scrolls orbiting him like papery comets trailing the dust of defunct philosophies. He changed. From summer to autumn, gold to bronze, foot to hoof. Words etched themselves across his flesh, runic scabby acrostics that read like Braille beneath my ink-stained fingertips. I no longer referred to him as my summer man. His hair became longer, darker, hanging in the air as if electrified. He contained all seasons, and depending on the text at hand, reflected them well. We had shared the poetry and chronicles of spring and summer, but winter lasts longest. I clung to his body as he recited from the books of the dead, his frosty fingertips tearing the pages, erasing names from history, men and women who are damned to exist only on his tongue and in my seared memory.

As we toured the endless chambers and tasted the world's literature, always the old men worked around us, carting away books or tirelessly rebuilding fallen stacks. I have grown to view them as mute librarians, a slavish network mining forgotten annals to rekindle memories. And I know now that if I had remained above ground, one day the old man at Metzengerstein Books and Magazines would have descended into the basement never to resurface. All would have been well, however, for I had been groomed to serve as his replacement.

The basement has proven a generous labyrinth with many exits. When I am able to tear myself away from him and push past the slavish librarians, I open the nearest available door. All lead to a bookstore at night. I can't stand to be parted from him for more than a few minutes, but these excursions to the surface remind me of the world I have abandoned: quaint dreams and notions, an innocence that smells of parchment and mold.

I've tiptoed through Parisian bookshops and startled their shabby cats. I've eaten cold pierogies left on a Russian counter and let the half-chewed food fall from my mouth, as I now survive on a steady diet of script and the inky soup of illuminated texts. I've been in all the shops along Charing

Cross Road. The stairs in Giovanni's Room, Philadelphia, creaked as I scrutinized their selection of Oscar Wilde, all the while coveting the memory of the unpublished priapic poems we'd discovered in the basement. I thought I was about to be surprised by a burglar, but no one was there. Once the door opened on to that favorite bookstore in the city where I had run into him so long ago. I was able to grab some pens and a notebook, and when I'm not reading or searching for forbidden knowledge, I've been able to write my story down. The next time I venture to the surface, I will slip this manuscript among the books on the shelf with the hope you will follow my advice and leave and never return.

THE CLOUD DRAGON ATE RED BALLOONS

The cloud dragon ate red balloons and was angry. That a beast of his stature should have to rend paltry rubber when soccer fields everywhere rolled with earnest boys...the dragon roiled in anguish. His very substance was forever buoyed above the morsel heads he craved, perpetually positioned with an excellent view of the denied buffet. The cloud dragon would hover over playgrounds and eviscerate himself into a thousand white feathers as blithe boys monkeyed on swings, obliviously competing to place their sandy toes within his ephemeral jaws. The wispy shards of his being would scatter in frustration to reconvene elsewhere, someplace principled and resolutely un-peopled, usually far above frosty seas or sober Alps. High in the stratosphere, the cloud dragon would assemble the shifting flakes of his scales. Drifting back toward land, coiling and uncoiling the mist of his long, reptilian shape in mute hostility, whiskers steaming, the dragon wished again for the weight of silver teeth.

❖

Most species of dragons had retired or, mistaken for dinosaurs, collectively hung their bones in museums, waiting in the wings for just the right time to reemerge, to scorch schools and char church parking lots. But cloud dragons were a harried lot. They were the first to drift away from the mind of the world. The tales that gave them ballast were forgotten; their untended shrines in remote Hokkaido had gone back to the earth. No one burned the incense that stroked their spines and blackened their brows. This particular cloud dragon had not met another of his race in centuries. As far as he knew, no other fantastical creatures combed the barren sky save the gargantuan cloud crustaceans.

The dragon steered clear of these miles-long lugubrious monstrosities. The gray rivets of their abdomens were a constant source of torrential rain. They were rumored to possess their own vaporous ecosystems containing clear koi fish that swam in the large pools of moisture which collected in the dimples of their shells, or snaky golden remoras that adhered to their bellies and flashed like distant lightning. But he had never bothered to investigate. Their sizeable pinchers made the otherwise impressive dragon feel like a wizened shrimp.

Japanese monks had deferentially joked with Western missionaries that cloud dragons were failed snow dragons that only had love for one another, never sharing their snow with Izanami, Mother Earth, and were thus unfettered, unproductive fantasies. The crawling pestilence of one religion consuming another was blight enough on the world, but the monks had disparaged the cloud dragons to mask the guilt of their own nightly assignations. That had only hastened the exodus of the creatures. Dragons of every rank and element abandoned the polluted islands just as they had previously divested the continents. They took to the oceans of the sky for convalescence.

❖

The cloud dragon, separated from his scaly flock and unsure if others still existed, directed his appetite toward the perky orbs of school boys on lonely country roads, delivering newspapers as dawn cracked its pink egg on the bowl of the horizon. The boys, in turn, mistook his seething drool for April showers. Condensation snaked down his winding body and darkened the tips of his curled claws as he skirted above the tinfoil globe of Flushing Meadows Park. He paused over an impromptu soccer game. Some of the running boys with shaved heads reminded him of the offending monks from long ago, and his stomach hungrily rumbled like a threatening storm, causing them to momentarily halt their game. They shielded their eyes to assess the risk of rain and, deciding the cloud above was of no consequence, continued to play. But those other boys reading alone under the trees sussed his shape. They saw the dragon as he truly was, though he himself did not know this. He did not know that they were trying to pull him down to earth with their inquisitive eyes—mouths open, eager for spring snow to melt on the red dagger of their extended tongues.

BLUE SEAWEED

PART I

Aeson beat the limp octopus against the sun-warmed rock until it was tender enough for his mother to cook. He chose this particular rock far from where the other boys assisted their fishermen-fathers in preparing the catch for market because of its shape and substance—obsidian and rectangular—a miniature altar that had absorbed the blood and ink from what he imagined must be centuries of sacrifice. He liked to imagine himself more a secret priest laboring at his sacrament than just another smelly boy turned away after his chores to bathe at the cistern. When he stared at the stains on the rock, he read them as a bloody alphabet he had yet to understand.

Barefoot and ankle-deep in the surf, Aeson whispered half-remembered prayers to Poseidon as he grabbed another octopus from the basket his father had passed him after a long day toiling on the wine-dark sea. He swung it against the rock with all his might. Purple ink splashed Aeson's loincloth. He swore and, dropping the octopus, dove into the water. No Roman, citizen or slave, could wear the color purple, a tint reserved for emperors only. Though far from Rome, Greece had been subjugated for so long that all the isles of the Aegean obeyed imperial edicts no matter how obscure. They were as ingrained as local superstitions, as prevalent as the abundant blue sky.

Golden sunlight flitted off the waves. Aeson rolled in the surf while the lucky octopus blossomed, tentacles uncurling as it danced nimbly toward the protection of the depths. Still not satisfied the ink had been thoroughly strained from his loincloth, he stripped and wrung it out several times, beating the fabric against the rock with more anger than he had ever administered to the poor octopi. Seawater splashed between his bare legs. The sun pressed against the young muscles of his shoulders. The other boys tended to their oceanic chores naked. Aeson rarely did so. Yet, rather than don the loincloth again, he laid it beside the basket with the remaining catch and waded back out. The sea felt safe and right. He labored in earnest as Apollo, more persistent then any mere octopus, stained the sky blood red. Soon the remaining clouds would unravel into the black veil of night.

Their island was the smallest of the Dodecanese islands—the destruction of the large dock during the Peloponnesian War was considered a blessing, as Imperial troops could no longer bivouac on their shores and deplete their supplies. The lone temple in the high hills of the island was ancient and overgrown with weeds, housing in its dark cellar a giant blind snake as old as the world itself. The serpent was cared for by a succession of sibyls. Aeson's father believed them to be old prostitutes who could not relinquish swindling shepherds.

Aeson's mother was not a Greek, though she possessed the same dark hair, olive skin, and a stare that could curdle milk into viper venom. Born in Carthage, a city larger than their island several times over, she raised her son with knowledge of other religions far beyond what the island folk possessed, though nothing she said contradicted respect for the sea. In many ways, what she said augmented it. Her thorough but humble knowledge of certain herbs that could soothe a woman's innards made her popular among the wives and mothers of the fisher-folk. She also knew much of Rome and could explain the moods of the incestuous gods in an offhand manner, as if discussing well-off neighbors.

She told Aeson the more flavorful details of empire and deity during their dawn excursions to the sea. It was common practice in his mother's homeland to trap octopi by placing clay pots in the shallows at sunset. The sleepy things curled within these containers for a night's rest and were trapped once the tide receded. He and his mother would retrieve the pots, thanking Selene of the moon. They kept this practice a secret because octopi were crafty creatures, and they feared if the entire village fished with pots the creatures would learn of the ruse and avoid the shore. All of which lent much to his father's reputation as an expert fisherman.

❖

Just before sunrise, Aeson jogged to the beach where he and his mother had secreted the pots. He did so alone, as this morning she complained of stomach pains, so she stayed behind. As much as he enjoyed their time together, the stories she weaved of Carthage, its temples, the many different people who filled its streets and plied their trades, he also liked being alone, marching down the beach like a centurion going into battle, the army of the night receding at his every formidable step.

The retreating tide revealed the rims of several pots. The first two were empty. One held a frustrated crab with meaty pinchers—a good find. His mouth watered at the thought of crab cakes and lentils. Within the last pot, a large octopus swirled. Regal in appearance, it spread its tentacles as if trailing a majestic robe. The pattern of its spots shifted across its flesh like rotating jewels. Aeson leaned in to study this remarkable creature. Besides its unique markings, something was different about it. Its eyes were human, clear, penetrating eyes, bold eyes, flashing curiosity.

He gripped the pot nervously. *There is no fear in these eyes*, he thought. By using the pots as a trap and watching his father fish, he had seen innumerable octopi confront death. The aquatic animals always treated death as if it were a puzzle to be solved and calmly wiggled out of traps, swiftly evaded nets and spears, or not. Their eyes betrayed a calculating nature that had always left Aeson cold but made his task of killing them much easier.

But this creature regarded him in the same manner that some of the older boys at the docks stared at him as he untangled nets. As he reached in to seize his catch, its eyes said the same thing the boys on the dock said: *soon.*

Long, low clouds peacefully unfurled across the horizon. Aeson took pity on his prey and overturned the pot to free the octopus. The creature stayed, however, and wavered in the shallows. A lone tentacle stretched out as if to brush his ankle, but instead the octopus shot off toward deeper waters like a hoplite's spear, trailing a wondrous cloud of ink. Aeson gathered the pots and brought the crab to his mother without a word about what had transpired. Later that day, when one of the older boys on the dock, Tycho, looked at him—Tycho whose shoulders were made wide by pulling the heaviest nets, the part of his black hair always shone blue in the noon sun—Aeson returned his stare with earnest curiosity. The boy smiled back.

The next morning, and for several mornings afterward, Aeson and his mother checked their traps. An abundance of octopi, urchins, and even large fish filled their tidal bowls. The additional catch enriched their kitchen as well as their returns at the market. His father gave assiduous thanks at Poseidon's altar and sacrificed the largest fish he caught to the god. When Aeson bowed and closed his eyes before the idols in the foyer of their small home, he envisioned the octopus peering at him. Not from the ocean, but from the clear blue sky. The image startled him, and he gave thanks to the gods for every fish caught as well as for the attention of Tycho, who now shared his bread every day and promised to teach him more about fishing.

When another morning found his mother ill, a problem Aeson was starting to realize had a pattern, he marched toward the shore early and alone. A few lingering stars still twinkled above. It intrigued him how the broken shells on the beach mingled with shards of pottery and other manmade detritus, how the remnants of humanity fit with that of nature. Some of the bits of pottery seemed as ancient as the conchs rolling in the surf. It almost dispelled the notion that the gods came first. He shook such blasphemy from his mind and headed toward the barely submerged pots, surprised to see another boy standing in the surf, naked, hands on his hips, as if impatiently awaiting his arrival.

Aeson knew the other youths of the island by sight, but this smiling youth beguiled him. He *was* familiar but he was not of the docks. His eyelashes were long and black and sharp like the needles of an urchin. Aeson noticed the boy's hair was black-green, a mass of seaweed above as well as below, and his underarms were webbed. This sea-boy possessed the perfect, lithe body of a sponge diver. An errant gull laughed overhead, and they both looked up and then at each other. The boy laughed, and Aeson recognized those intelligent eyes.

By Poseidon, it can't be, he thought, and he took several steps back toward home.

"It's good to see you again." The sea-boy's voice sounded as if it were coming from miles away, underwater, from beneath other islands distant and covered with white sand. Aeson blushed and turned his chin into his shoulder, about to reflexively whisper a prayer of protection he'd learned from his mother, African words he didn't understand, sounds alien to Grecian shores but maternally comforting nonetheless.

"There's no need for incantations." The youth stepped closer. "I've all the magic you need. Your act of charity freed me, and I am here to repay you in full."

Aeson fell to his knees. The sea-boy knelt beside him in the loam and brushed the hair out of his moist eyes. The Aegean came to a rest. No waves crashed. The clouds froze in the sky. For a child of the gods to declare he owed a mortal a debt was something of myth. Aeson kept his eyes on the rock where he knelt. "Are you cursed? Or do you change shape like the surf?"

The sea youth laughed high. "I can bite like a shark, swim like a dolphin, and pinch your feet like a crab." He made a dodge and tickle at Aeson's calves. The boy reflexively flinched, all the while marveling that this demigod was playful rather than haughty.

More questions were about to stumble out when the sea-boy rose up on the surprise of a wave, silvery foam decorating his shoulders like medallions. The clouds above began to roll again. Aeson stammered, concerned he'd lost a precious moment that he needed to ask for a prosperous life and a great catch every day for his father and eternal beauty for his mother, but the boy from the sea pressed his full lips to Aeson's, followed by a whisper, tongue lilting on earlobe.

"And I kiss like a seahorse."

As the subsequent wave washed over them, the godling vanished. Aeson was left drenched, astounded that the kiss stung like a jellyfish. It could not be forgotten.

Part II

The boys each hid behind the gnarled trunk of a dark cypress tree and tried to become one with the shadows. Aeson forgot who among their rangy pack had first dared them to spy on the temple, but as night descended, he was sure it was one of the youths who had abandoned the quest once it had been decided on in earnest. Some declared a bit too loudly that they would be severely beaten if they were late for another dinner, ensuring they would be teased mercilessly for days afterward. The smart ones simply slinked away once the silent march through the hills had commenced. All along the dusty trail, with every turn that afforded them a moment of privacy, Tycho would brush his hand against Aeson's rear. His friendship with Tycho had gained him acceptance among the boys who worked the nets. If any of these new friends witnessed this casual contact, it was easy to assume it was incidental to their steep climb, but Aeson knew it was an insistent invitation to continue their recent play beneath the docks. Several of the boys had paired off into friendships that moved from wrestling and horseplay to erotic interlockings and then back again, all tugged by a silent tide he could not gauge. Whenever they were alone and the mood struck Tycho, he would hook his arm roughly around Aeson's neck, puff out his chest and close his eyes, signaling for Aeson to kiss his way downward and taste the awaiting salt.

❖

Once they had ascended the hills, an earnest quietude settled among them. Only the obnoxious Pamphilos had been to the temple before, necessitating his begrudged participation. The tax collector's son, he had inherited his father's contemptible reputation, lean frame, and premature hunch. However, having traversed the island with his father, he knew the terrain better than anyone his age and was able to guide them swiftly through the scary copse of bare trees surrounding the temple. Stars were already alight as the hills below dripped with darkness. Aeson took a quick head count: another boy or two had held back and scampered away. Their smaller numbers had sapped the bravery and bravado that usually kept the group jostling and challenging one another. Now they moved through the sparse, gray forest as separate, silent animals, more potential prey than bold hunting party.

The laughter of women was startling. Somehow he had expected solemn sacrifices, something closer to his bloody but unresolved daydreams of Tycho leering over him, holding a knife, punishing him with little cuts for never once asking him to return the favor. At night, these images led to arousal. He reached for Tycho and recoiled at finding a boney, damp hand.

"Don't jump, Aeson, it's only me," Pamphilos sneered. "Bet you thought it was Tycho. He's over there, trying to get a better look. Honestly, I don't know what you see in that brute."

Aeson fumed and was about to protest when the boy continued, "Well, I know what you swallow! Don't be mad, half the village has drunk from that spigot. It's worth it just to watch how his eyes drop to half-mast as his ship's about to make port."

Speechless, confused, he wanted to defend Tycho but recalled how the older boy always casually patted him on the neck when he was done, as if he were nothing more than a pup.

Never a kiss.

"Oh, apologies. I see you thought you were, what? Special to him? He's a fisherman, Aeson. He casts a wide net."

"And I bet you've been dragged through the sand by more than just him." As soon as he said it, Aeson felt defeated, drawn into a meaningless quarrel on a night meant for starry mysteries.

Pamphilos ignored the comment and looked him steadily in the eyes.

"The real question, Aeson, is why we go for boys like that and shun the ones just like us." He spoke ruefully, not only to Aeson but to other men in other ages. Aeson blinked, not really understanding.

"Oh come on, surely you saw the play *Myrmidon* by Aeschylus when that last threadbare batch of actors made port."

Aeson shook his head.

"Well, *I* remember your mother scratching the alphabet in the sand for you, when we were both little boys, Aeson, while other parents were content to let their brats play knucklebones with bits of coral. She taught you to read for a *reason*. Come by my house. Father has *his* father's scroll of the *Symposium*. Both were educated in Athens, you know," he sniffed.

Aeson knew. The whole island knew, as Pamphilos never tired of repeating it. And he *had* been reading. His mother had several scrolls in a variety of languages, and he pored over all them, but especially the ones concerning mythology. And the sea. He burned to understand the gods, and, in particular, how mortals gained their attention. But now he wondered if he might not turn his attention to the world of men. And women. The laughter from within the temple stilled. The fire within darkened, and more smoke poured out. Rich smoke, powerful incense. The leaves above rustled and two dark shapes slipped away hand in hand back through the forest. Aeson looked for Tycho. Pamphilos stifled a cough. That sour boy had nonchalantly shredded his world while hinting at a more complex, satisfying one.

Smoke wound around the cypress trees. It was getting harder to see. He wanted to whisper to Pamphilos that they should join the others and depart, but a procession of women emerged from the now-dark temple. The women carried incense and amphoras of libation, both for the unnamed gods they served as well as themselves. Aeson was shocked to see the women were of different classes, fisherwives and the snootiest of merchant matrons. Prostitutes walked side by side with the youngest, virginal women of the island. Even Pamphilos's sisters took part. Younger than him, they already possessed the same defeated shoulders.

Aeson gasped as the procession parted for his mother. She walked deliberately, holding aloft the head of the giant snake that lived beneath the shrine. Several veiled women struggled with the length and tail of the serpent. The boy peered through the gloom to see his mother was face-to-face with the giant reptile, that it glittered in the darkness as if born of the night, and that its rhythmic movements were not in protest of being removed from its earthen lair, but judging by the flicker of its tongue and the familiar smile that crossed his mother's pale-in-the-moonlight face, they had just shared a joke both private and universal.

PART III

As their modest island was the runt of the Dodecanese chain, Rhodes was the largest, and this was where Aeson failed to make his fortune as a tutor. One night, exhausted from constant hunger, he leaned against the ancient base of the broken statue of Colossus, a fine and ironic symbol of his own short-lived dreams snapped off at the ankles. The monolith had stood guard over the port, seemingly permanent and strong, and had lasted scant fifty or so years before tumbling into the sea during a ferocious earthquake. So, too, had Aeson's dreams crumbled into dust shortly after his arrival on Rhodes. The base of the statue maintained the feet and cracked ankles of the Colossus only. The rest of the giant lay beneath the waves of the harbor. Aeson wished to join these pieces and had spent the last of his paltry dupondius on a considerable amount of harsh wine to strengthen his resolve.

Several prostitutes reclined between the orbs of the massive heels where countless men and boys had chiseled their marks in a vain attempt to be remembered long after they had passed. The Colossus's toenails had been painted white by a century's worth of seagull guano. The whores ignored

Aeson. They appreciated a drunk's resolve but could smell when a man had already spent his earnings. A few of the boys plying their trade lingered nearby, hiking up their tunics and making lewd gestures as if to encourage him to find more coin. Aeson thought they looked like emaciated sharks.

Jugglers had set up shop nearby and, thinking a sulking scholar would be bad for business, kept giving him the evil eye. He shoved off and stumbled toward the rocky shore. The glow of cooking fires and lamp light illuminated the city of Rhodes and lent it an urbane air, but he knew better. Things had begun to go wrong when Pamphilos had abandoned him just as their ship was to set sail. He listed a litany of excuses, but Aeson knew he had fallen head over heels for a blond shepherd boy of late. For all his vaunted discourse of the philosophies of love, he was forever smitten with men who worked the fields or fished the ocean. So they parted without protestation on Aeson's part.

The voyage to Rhodes had been marred by stormy seas, and he'd found no tranquility on land. The languages his mother had taught him had made him a star pupil on their island, but he was just another peddler of lessons on Rhodes. Up against sharper tutors from Rome and beyond, he had been cheated, beaten, and thwarted at every turn by employers, nasty merchants, and conniving landlords. He made a sign of protection, and not one familiar to the Greek and Roman populace of the island, but a secret one taught to him by his mother. The thought of her and how disappointed she would be spurred him on toward the black water.

A bleak and forlorn sea, cold without Apollo's caress, faced him. Aeson stumbled as a wave urged him back to shore. He tried to think of a fitting Homeric quote, something stoic, about Hector breaking horses, to lend his death dignity, but instead he coughed as his stomach shot a flaming arrow of bile up his throat. Water licked his ankles and sand sucked at his sandals, and all he could think of was some drivel attributed to Martial he had gleaned from a bathhouse wall:

The whores here are like sellers of fish
The earlier you arrive, the fresher the dish

Even while walking toward a watery Hades, he couldn't summon up a decent poem—failure marked his every move. The tide took a sandal, so he shucked its mate, and as his dirty toga floated about his waist, he undid that as well. Best to face his end as naked as he was born, though he worried that the effect the chilly water was having on his manhood would follow him into the afterlife. Would the other shades be dressed and mock him for dying naked? He turned to fetch his toga, but it had already rolled toward shore with the waves. To slosh after it would be a show of weakness, another retreat toward a city that had shown him only bitter pain.

He turned back toward open sea, wanting, deserving oblivion and found himself face-to-face with a pink porpoise. The mercurial mammal regarded him with knowing eyes, and Aeson raised his hand to sign against evil spirits as a large wave lifted him. Black water filled his mouth as he flailed his arms in protest. The next wave pushed his head under, and he heard the porpoise cluck an eager greeting. The bile that laced his throat coated his mouth in a belch of wine as the kind creature nudged him upward, nose prodding his armpit, until Aeson was treading water.

Another wave obscured his view of the island, and he was alone with the porpoise. The stars burned in the firmament as he swam with this magical beast in the shifting ocean. It glistened, a thing of joyful grace, permanent puckish grin affixed to its long snout. He clung to it for security, and as the next wave lifted them, he saw the harbor was quite close. He could hear the laughter of whores and smell skewers of burning meat. The porpoise chirruped and familiar eyes locked on his. He was struck dumb. The porpoise nodded, and Aeson knew to tighten his grip as the next wave crested and together they disappeared beneath the water.

The rush of water sobered him, the darkness below all consuming until his eyes adjusted and the dim glow of coral and the distant bloom of jellyfish began to match the stars above in their twirling brilliance. He held on to his living chariot as they descended farther into the deep. The salt stung his eyes but still he could make out the corroded wrecks of slave galleons and the dunes of silt that forged the valley of the harbor. A mirror of flashing silverfish hung above tall strands of seaweed. The air in his lungs was nearly depleted. Pain filled his chest. He wanted to push against the pink animal and return to the surface, but he knew only failure waited there. Something more was in store for him below the sea, if he survived the plunge. Aeson closed his eyes as the ache in his lungs surged, and when he opened them he felt as if all were lost. The giant cobalt hand of Hades reached out to beckon him toward hell. A last resilient bubble of air escaped from between his lips before he realized it wasn't the god of the Underworld but the errant arm of the collapsed Colossus nestled in the sand, fingers outstretched as if to welcome him home.

❖

The reverberating echo of dripping water splintered his hangover into a hundred shards of ignoble regret. He clutched his forehead and thought to call for Rufus, the household slave who had lost an arm in the Battle of Samarra, to bring him something to drink, but remembered he had been relieved of employment the day before. Startled at the thought that he wasn't in his quarters, yet somehow sleeping off a good drunk as it rained outside, he lurched awake only to find that it was raining inside his skull. No, not his skull, *someone else's*. He was just a guest here, inside a vast cranium of saturated thought.

He sat for a long moment trying to reconcile his surroundings: the great orb that contained him, the glittering pool of seawater, and the small island of sand and coral he occupied. Two encrusted alcoves, a reversal of gigantic eyes on either side of the hollow of a masculine nose supported by a crisscross of rusting balustrades. Nude, Aeson rested on the sand, inside the fallen head of the Colossus of Rhodes.

An orange crab scampered by, and he tucked his feet beneath him. Granules of sand dug into his pores, and his eyes stung from the salt-rich air. A lush array of coral crept up the internal walls of the decapitated head while swords of rust plunged downward toward the clear water that gathered at the back of its head. Giant incandescent pearls were strung throughout, illuminating this underwater oasis. The severed neck was tilted just so. It must have lodged on the rocks or other giant bits of statue, creating a bubble of air within the cranium. A slim crevice above the sand that poured through the neck acted like the mouth of a cave. It was through this dark opening that the boy with green hair emerged.

Aeson fell to his knees, a shaking supplicant to what was obviously a god. The lithe boy's skin shimmered, the same texture of the pink porpoise, though now his flesh was golden, like Aeson's used to be when he fished with his father. Now his limbs were pale from spending too much time in libraries.

Prostrate, he cried out to Poseidon as the divinity rested a warm hand on the nape of his neck and calmed him with a whispered denial.

"I am not Poseidon, and have yet to meet my grandfather."

Aeson recognized the silky voice from that one morning many years ago.

"I am Triton, but not *the* favored Triton, whom I have also never met. Both gods have laced the ocean with their seed like randy seahorses, so much so that Poseidon's eldest stopped naming his sea-whelps. We are all his little Tritons, squirming prongs from the end of his prodigious trident, no doubt."

Triton stood before Aeson and held out his hand. Strands of blue seaweed draped over his palm. This kelp was exceptional. It was the shifting color of light piercing the deepest parts of the ocean. Aeson realized he was starving and ate from Triton's proffered hand, looking up at the godling as a dog would eye its master. Triton smiled, took him by the hand, and helped him stand. Aeson marveled at the changes that had begun to take hold of his body. He felt refreshed and strong. Skin now golden brown, he felt ready for the Olympics. He stammered in gratitude and again bowed before the godling, but Triton clucked his tongue and held Aeson's hand as they strolled around the tiny sparkling atoll within the head of the Colossus.

"It is I who should show gratitude toward you. That day on the beach, if you hadn't rescued me from the pot but exposed my full form to the elements of earth and air, I would have remained an octopus and likely been someone's dinner, maybe yours!"

Triton looked him in the eyes, searching for the answer to an as-yet-unasked question. "I knew I would see you again, but not under such dour circumstances. If life above is so hard, then I implore you to live below the sea. Here you will find much wonderment and adventure, and most important, here you will find me."

They kissed, and Aeson felt his lips swell as if stung once more by a jellyfish. Triton held him in his arms, which expanded and multiplied into the arms of an octopus, kissing his flesh everywhere and all at once. Aeson held on to the godling as they tumbled into the water. Locked in a tight embrace, they rolled about as wavering strands of blue seaweed wrapped around them to form a shared and flowing royal robe. Halos of silver fish encircled them as Triton took the form of a pink porpoise and Aeson mounted him. They rode out from within the head of the Colossus to review the coral gardens and sandy vales of his new home.

DIABOLICAL

The Devil was masturbating on my train.
I didn't notice him when I boarded the A train from the lonely downtown stop. I was just happy to have my choice of seats. Only after I had nestled in did I see the Devil. Always depicted as fiery red, his skin was orchid purple, as rich and tawdry as the dark drapes of a dilapidated porn theater.

I was drawn to him. I wanted to kneel before him and examine his lush, velveteen flesh.

The Devil moaned. Opening and closing his fists, he slid farther back into his seat opposite me. We were alone in the car as the train rocketed uptown. I watched as he ejaculated black semen onto the floor of the rollicking subway car. Flammable oil oozed from the glistening, cloven tip of his penis, which quickly deflated, slithering back, coiling like the first serpent into a nest of riled, electrified pubic hair. The sulfuric cum repelled even itself and scattered loudly, onyx marbles in every direction across the filthy floor.

He winked at me as I pulled my shopping bags closer.
I blushed.

The Devil shifted his position in my direction. Renewed arousal: his foreskin slowly withdrew to again reveal the pink snake's tongue of his slight crown. The Devil was not well-endowed in the typical sense, though what he lacked in girth, he more than made up for in length. His penis was meant to peek through keyholes, sneak around corners, tap you on the shoulder and snatch your wallet from out of your pants pocket when you turned.

I absentmindedly felt for my wallet as he smiled a volcanic grin. His teeth were the shade of spent charcoal briquettes.

The train hissed to a stop. Doors automatically opened, momentarily cleansing the subway car of sulfuric stench. No one boarded. As the doors closed, I caught a quick glimpse of the station: lengthy, twisting stalactites hung from the ceiling, penetrating the cracked tiled floor. A peeling ad for a pitchfork sharpener hung above an ornate, gothic bench. We were much farther underground than I'd have thought possible.

I felt the air grow hotter; the Devil was hitting on me.

I self-consciously spread my legs and ground my buttocks against the warm seat. One of my shopping bags dropped as I straightened a leg to better accommodate the erection trapped between the tightness of my threadbare jeans and sweaty thigh.

He sat upright and sniffed the air while parting his legs. Surprise. No hooves. A blast of black hair scratched the top of his long, slender simian feet—finger-like digits shone, bejeweled with corn-colored diamond toenails. An additional dagger-like toe adhered to each heel. These feet could shake your hand, deal poker, pour tea, button a coat, and cut a throat.

A nugget of black semen rolled my way. It bounced as the train took a turn. Coming to rest against my sneaker, it caught fire. In an instant, my clothes disintegrated within a smokeless aura of blue flame.

Embarrassed, now naked and fully aroused, dripping with sweat, I glared at the Devil. He just shrugged.

I desperately wanted the Devil and imagined how his forked tongue would divide itself on the curvature of my dick,

its unearthly grip delivering the ecstasy of the underworld—
the weapon that had unhinged countless hearts and upended
nations would grovel over *my* sex. I rose and approached. He
flexed his thighs and spread his arms across the back of his seat.
The train dipped more downward still. From between shiny,
alien knees, his cock writhed. Leathery foreskin stretched,
steam rose. He parted his black lips in anticipation, but I stood
my ground and held my dick out. He exhaled and arched an
eyebrow, amused. I'm guessing not that many people tease the
Devil. Arctic fingers slowly encircled my engorged cock.

When the Devil spoke—"I am yours"—the train halted.

Silence overwhelmed. I was beyond the precipice of
seduction and holding steady.

His eyes shone like candlelight off an ancient bronze
shield depicting a multitude of agonies. "And when we reach
your subway stop, you are mine."

I've always said I clean up well. Obviously unbeknownst
to His Satanic Majesty, these shopping bags held my few
belongings: soiled clothes, some paperbacks, and an old
toothbrush. I like to meet guys in a bar late at night so staying
over seems natural, showering after sex obvious, rummaging
through their fridge casual and right. But tonight, I didn't score
and had planned to just sleep on the train.

I returned his intense gaze with real longing and a fear
more manufactured than felt.

"Sure."

My hand on the back of his reptilian neck, the train started
to move again as I planned on taking my time. I had all the
infernal time in the world.

The Ice King

The Ice King walked into the Bear Trap off Twelfth Avenue and stood, allowing the patrons hunkered at the bar to size him up. He liked to be admired. The men mostly looked like him, overly masculine, large, and in leather. Several shaved heads wrapped in aviator glasses regarded him, and though he revealed no obvious emotion, the Ice King knew he was lusted after. He always was.

Music pulsed. A few men pretending to be bored lifted drinks. Under the red lights, the alcohol in the bottom of their glasses shone like diluted, bloody mucus. He stepped up to the bar and placed a boot on the rail. Men in jackets and leather pants turned to exhibit their hard-won physiques. The Ice King's chiseled musculature was strapped by a leather-studded harness that crossed his chest and back, buckling at the waist of his leather chaps. Everyone was dressed like him in his own way, but no one else wore gloves. Cracking his knuckles produced an icy vapor imperceptible in the darkness of the bar.

When he takes off his gloves, people die at his frozen touch.

The Ice King put a leather finger to his mustache and smoothed his upper lip. He was thirsty, but not for alcohol. Under natural light, it would have been more noticeable that his skin was completely white, but he was not an albino. He *was* ice. Flesh steely, like a distant mountain peak, cold and lifeless rock beneath the permanent tundra. Metallic blue pupils swirled around white irises. His arctic gaze could freeze anyone and anything.

The bartender eyed him wearily, but the Ice King ignored him, absently stroking the long scar that marred his perfect bicep. The memory of that battle, the particular superhero who'd administered the punishment bordering on total defeat, filled him with anger. And anger led to arousal.

He exhaled frozen breath. *The fools probably think I'm smoking.* He puckered and blew lazy smoke rings of chilled air toward the ceiling. A fair-haired twink sashayed by, giving him a long look. He had always liked blonds.

The boy cocked his hips as he walked, ridiculously tight vinyl pants shivered low across his shapely ass. He paused at the stairwell to the basement and looked back at the Ice King, his parted lips glossy, feminine. The Ice King followed. The music wasn't as oppressively loud toward the back of the bar. The lights were fewer. No one noticed the icy vapor rising from the snowy footprints he left on the floor. Numerous bars throughout the world were named the Bear Trap. The only thing they had in common was the type of men they attracted: ready and willing. Likely he had been to all of them. He couldn't remember the layout of this one, though, and he relished the anticipation welling up within. It was rare that any emotion broke through his permafrost of disdain.

He descended the stairs into a labyrinthine bathroom of doorless stalls and leaky urinals. A fluorescent tube hung askew from the ceiling and flickered weakly. The stale air stank of piss and cheap poppers and cigarette smoke. Now he remembered; there *was* a back room. The broom closet concealed a gross curtain that led to an ancient basement, practically a cave, with an earthen floor to soak up the sweat and semen of desperate animal assignations. The Ice King stepped into the antechamber crowded with mops rancid from the sour scent of bleach. He could hear men panting, sucking, and wallowing in the darkness. These men were the clay he would sculpt.

In bathhouses and backrooms, he fashioned icy atrocities when the mood struck, orchestras of men frozen in acts of fellatio, masturbating strange flowers of arrested sperm arcing in the air, mouths opened in screams of ecstasy or death, stalactites of sweat hanging off their chins. First he would observe the men, pushing away any who approached so he could better study the action of the room. And when the men reached a crescendo he thought aesthetically pleasing, he would take off his gloves and touch the nearest coupling.

Walking through the room, he spread winter. All froze, and he would pause by the door and exhale a final, wintry blast of satisfaction. Art wrongly considered a crime when discovered. He knew his vision was unappreciated by the masses, much less the authorities. Still, his only hope was that the police photographers accurately captured his work and preserved it for future generations. Possibly when the sun had dimmed, and the world had grown colder—became a bit more like *him*—only then would his work gain the recognition it deserved.

The twink stepped from the shadows. The Ice King had seen enough. He grabbed the boy roughly by the back of his hair and jerked his mouth open. The boy gasped in surprise but fumbled eagerly for the Ice King's zipper. They kissed and the temperature in the room suddenly dropped. He savored the swirl of fear and excitement in the boy's eyes and watched closely as they became cloudy with frost.

Winter came.

❖

The Ice King slowly rose above the city on a cloud of ice particles. With minimal concentration, he could successively freeze and unfreeze the moisture in the air in such a way as to propel him to serious heights at great speed. Obscured by clouds, he traveled the world, delivering icy mayhem wherever he pleased. The cold hell he'd created in the back room at the Bear Trap should have given him immense pleasure, but he was left wanting. The scar on his arm ached as he considered its source, the Canadian hero, Light Stream. The one time they had grappled, Light Stream prevailed. Yet as the embodiment of cold, the Ice King considered himself a harbinger of death, so rather than feel defeated, he felt challenged. He was drawn to the earnestness of Light Stream, though usually revolted by such sincerity. Coming from the hero, it seemed wistful and also oddly familiar. The Ice King wanted to return the touch, leave his own scars before freezing the blood in those "heroic" veins. The way his long hair had whipped about his face as they fought, hand-to-hand, high in the sky… He had always liked blonds.

A new destination fixed in his mind, he turned and flew north over the city. Sirens wailed below. The Empire State Building stung the low clouds. Appropriately, the landmark was lit white. Snow white.

❖

Mother Bear lived in a simple cabin on an island off the coast of Maine. She owned the island, as well as property in the Rocky Mountains. She often shared the island with the occasional girlfriend, though Mother Bear was short-tempered, and her lovers never lasted long. Mother Bear was one of those mutants the government worried so much about. Worse, she was fully dedicated to realizing their worst fears.

As the founder of the Annihilators, she attempted to forge a group to counter the World Guardians. Where the Guardians strove to ease the world's ills, the Annihilators worked to both spread and benefit from chaos. Unfortunately, the other Annihilators were jailed or dead. Only Mother Bear had escaped and, though she quietly scoured the world for new villains to re-assemble her team, she was battle-weary. She spent more and more time in bear-form, scavenging in the woods, fishing with her paws in streams, or napping in dark caves. Of the villains she had originally approached, the Ice King was the only one who had refused to join *and* survived her formidable anger at being rebuffed. His cold fortitude had earned him her respect, and then begrudging friendship.

He landed on her island. Frost from his dispersing cloud mingled with the morning mist and painted a thick mat of pine needles white. The island was covered with pine trees. The rocky ground never really leveled, slowing any approach to the cabin. The cabin was built into a hill, one side on stilts, with firewood stored beneath. He listened carefully as he approached but heard only birdsong. Smoke rose from the chimney. She was home. He formed a snowball in the palm of his hand and lobbed it at a window—a direct hit. He saw movement, and the window swung open. Mother Bear pushed the hair out of her eyes and gave him a casual wave. A rare smile cracked his face.

She was still pulling on a pair of old jeans as he entered the cabin. Her door was always unlocked. This was her island, and anyone who entered uninvited did so at great peril. The cabin was one big room, toasty from the fire in the fireplace. She immediately opened more windows to cool the room on his behalf, and then she walked over to give him a great big bear hug. The constant cold that radiated from his flesh never bothered her; bears can naturally withstand low temperatures. He relaxed and fell into an old recliner. A four-poster bed under a jumble of flannel sheets consumed one whole corner. The walls were lined by shelves stocked with necessities. The floor was carpeted with deerskin rugs, animals Mother Bear had hunted and killed herself. A giant freezer stretched beside an equally large refrigerator. She offered him coffee, black. He took the mug and blew on it until it was perfectly chilled. He realized he was jet-lagged and malnourished; he hadn't slept or eaten in days.

"Your handiwork made the news." She blew on her own steaming cup of coffee and nodded toward the television. When she wasn't rambling in the woods for days on end, Mother Bear was glued to the television. She was a news junkie, constantly channel surfing for news of unexplained phenomena that might help her locate new, hopefully malicious mutants. And she devoured true crime paperbacks. He often teased her over her choice of literature, yet he relished the facts she would spout about serial killers and Nazis.

"Yes, it was one of my better sculpture gardens." He yawned.

"You look famished, dear. I'm making stew." The light aroma of which had just reached him.

Dirty hiking boots much too small for Mother Bear stood idle by the door. A bloody bone protruded from one. He eyed her. "Oh, you didn't."

"Well, she couldn't play cards worth a damn, and I was getting hungry." She exaggeratedly licked her lips and smiled.

The Ice King let out a short chortle. "You and your girlfriends. You'll never settle down."

She lifted the spoon to her lips and blew. "Yes, I'm

something of a nomad, but not as much as you. I can tell this is just a stopover. What are you planning?"

His eyelids grew heavy. "Something big, something really, really big." He yawned.

Sleep was an impending avalanche of shadows.

❖

The Ice King woke in total darkness. It was well past midnight, and the cabin was still. Through the open window, stars were visible in the night sky. He felt rested and ready to leave but knew that would be rude. Not that Mother Bear would mind, but he hadn't come all this way just to power nap. She snored and shifted under a mound of blankets.

He put his hands behind his head. Mother Bear was a large woman, what people would call "big-boned." Crooked teeth and a man's chin were softened only by the thick brown hair that curled to her waist. Reading glasses also made her look less dangerous, more librarian than carnivore. Yet, besides himself, she was the most treacherous criminal he knew. Likely they were drawn together because they were equally misunderstood. While often labeled "psychopaths," each had a natural understanding of what other people were to them: prey.

The room was still lightly scented from the stew. Though he didn't eat as much of it as she did—no one could put away food like Mother Bear—he savored the rawness of the undercooked meat and the naturalness of the sparsely used herbs and spices she had caringly gathered from the woodlands of her island. Both had laughed when she had momentarily gagged and then spat out a human tooth.

When the Ice King reflected on the difference between himself and others of the super-powered elite, one singular factor emerged: determination. Mutants were a genetic crapshoot, some with a less-than-fortunate outcome. None had purposefully sought power as the Ice King had. He had struggled in the industry of cryogenics. His willingness to experiment and take risks was frowned upon by the very management poised to reap profits from the outcome. The brightest are always managed by the dim, the weary, and the weak. He was once weak. So he trained his body as he had trained his mind, consistently toward the twin goals of strength and success.

In his experiments, he asked himself a simple question. *If we can preserve a dead body by lowering its temperature, why not find a way to strengthen a living being with the same principles?* He thought it was ludicrous and limited that his field was focused solely on conservation and not enhancement. Revolutionary ideas are often dismissed as the ravings of madmen, so he kept quiet. He needed equipment and chemicals and research subjects, not peer approval. He still savored the memory of blowing out the windows of the laboratory.

Shocked employees gathered in the parking lot. They thought the clouds smoke, the initial snow, ash. They were perplexed when they saw their breath. When the first frozen corpse of a security guard was hurled onto the pavement below, shattering like an icicle, they ran for their cars. He laughed as they fled. Testing his new powers, he conjured blasts of icy wind strong enough to rip through the elevator doors and sever the suspending cables, dropping those trapped within to their doom. Going from office to office, he killed at random. Laughing, he commanded swirls of snow and ice to shoot from his hands and coat every surface. Desks turned into giant ice cubes. And if a luckless secretary huddled beneath it, so be it. He had made no friends at the company. That thought, in particular, had made him howl in delight. Everyone had called him the "ice queen," and not always behind his back. Now he had showed them he was, indeed, made of ice. *He* was in control, *he* was the strong one. A thin layer of ice frost covered his skin and hardened against the words, the snickering—he was finally, truly, impenetrably, cold.

Mother Bear shifted in her bed. The Ice King squinted, trying to discern what shape she had taken. Often she slept in bear form. The most peculiar aspect of her transformation was that when she shifted, her animal form was male. Functionally male. Size-wise, *impressively* male. A massive furry paw kicked the covers away. The Ice King rose from the recliner and thought, *Isn't it dangerous to disturb a sleeping bear?* He took a running jump and dove into the bed. Mother Bear, annoyed, desolately roared. She swiftly pinned him, baring her teeth less than an inch from his face. He pulled on her fur. She batted him roughly until he rolled on his stomach. The claw marks that marred his back from their last encounter were permanent. He relished the scars, loved that she could cut through his icy layers. Her rising girth threatened his buttocks. She slashed his leather jockstrap to ribbons and bore down with all her weight. A mighty roar shook the nearby trees, overshadowing his whimpers of delight.

❖

Light Stream flew high over Lake St. Claire. The sight of the desolate, choppy waters below cleared his mind. Though he spent most of his time flying between Vancouver and the newly erected headquarters of the World Guardians in New York, he relished his trips to Toronto. He loved the height of the city, and like the residents there, he thought of it as a cleaner, more civilized Manhattan. And the Great North. To be able to dive off the top of CN Tower and rush across the mountains and over untouched forest was the only thing that made him feel at peace. Here, Light Stream was able to free himself from the confines of the word "hero." Sometimes he thought if he ever wore a cape, he would wrap it around his neck and choke himself. Of all the members of the World Guardians, he was the only one who seemed to *live* the mission. The others shed all responsibilities when they took off their masks. Well, he didn't wear a mask. He was through with masks.

In high school and college, well after he knew he had been blessed with the ability to fly and bend light, he never dared use his powers. He never acted on his desire to soar, to snap his fingers and spin lightning into the air. No, it took him a long time to know who he was and why he was here. That left no room for masks. His costume was designed strictly for aerodynamics. He had purposefully chosen a dark purple to help pilots see him at a great distance. His hair was long simply because he never thought to get it cut. He didn't think of himself as handsome and was amused by how the press portrayed him as vainglorious. As a flock of geese changed direction to avoid him, he banked low, giving them plenty of room.

As he flew close to the lake, spray from the choppy water flecked his face. Whenever he was alone, feeling the pressures of his chosen path, he compulsively reviewed those moments in his earlier life when he had failed to grapple with his problems, the opportunities he had let slip away, needs that had gone unexpressed and unfulfilled. He remembered his first college roommate. They were both the skinniest boys in the dorm, the bespectacled outcasts. All they had in common should have bound them together, but they never formed a friendship, rarely spoke beyond the bland pleasantries demanded by their shared space. Yet at night, from the bottom bunk, Light Stream could tell when his roommate was pretending to sleep, that they both were awake, aware of their barely clothed bodies yearning to be touched. But they only touched once, the last night of the semester. After summer break, he returned to the dorm room having stored up the courage to confront his roommate about their mutual inclinations, only to find the other boy had transferred to another college without so much as a good-bye. It was something he had always regretted, yet the moment was a catalyst. At that point, he decided to live deliberately and plot his difficult destiny.

He rose slightly to avoid a buoy and decided to head back to the city. *But which one? Wherever I decide to go, there will be a problem I need to solve, an emergency to tackle. And wherever I don't visit, a crime will be committed.* Funny, now that he had finally come to terms with his powers and had dedicated his life to public service, gained the rock-hard body such training and discipline demanded, he still found himself attracted to the youngish, thin men who sheepishly asked for his autograph, their intelligence and interest shining through their thick glasses. He knew his nervousness at their proximity came off as typical superhero aloofness. This, in turn, fueled their worshipful deference, meaning he slept alone most nights and, when in Manhattan, was forced to dine out with whatever character from the World Guardians happened to be available.

Just as he turned north, he noticed an unusual glimmer from within a dark cloud over Detroit. Even though he had flown all over the continent, he still found it unusual that an oddity of geography placed Detroit north of parts of Canada. The black cloud was stationary over the city. Light seemingly reflected off a new skyscraper from within, impressive at even such a distance. Light Stream decided to investigate.

I don't remember seeing a new skyscraper the last time I flew over Detroit. And Detroit was a shrinking city. It had lost population in the seventies and never recouped. Its crime rate made him a repeat visitor. New construction of this magnitude and speed was unbelievable.

Instinctively, Light Stream again flew low to camouflage his approach. He slowed his speed to better assess the situation, and as he did so, the hero noticed a considerable dip in the temperature. Large chucks of ice started to crowd the waters below.

But it's only September.

He was close enough to discern that the Marriott hotel, the tallest building in the city, had been engulfed by ice. Frozen towers shot up into the air, so much ice that the massive complex of skyscrapers known as the Renaissance Center surrounding the hotel was consumed as well. Light Stream hovered and shivered, gripping his thick shoulders. He marveled at the giant crystal castle, which was nearly a work of art. But within the frozen turrets, he noticed little black dots. He floated closer. People. A man with a briefcase. A woman still in her robe frozen in mid-leap as she tried to escape the surging cold by jumping out of her hotel room window.

The Ice King.

Light Stream's frame glowed with an angry light. His powers roiled, and halos of angry sparks ignited around his wrists. Immediately, he soared upward and sought a defensive position in the clouds. Just as the Ice King had planned. The blow from behind was powerful. The impact knocked the breath out of him. Light Stream exhaled and folded and would have fallen except for the cold arms that embraced him. Consciousness flickered, and for a moment, he relaxed into the arms gripping his chest. The clouds were sheets and pillows, and this was the way he wanted to wake up in the morning, caressed lightly, strong arms around him, protecting him, loving him. But the embrace was cold. The dull burn of frostbite bit through his costume. He was revived, but at a loss. *Why hasn't the Ice King tried to kill me?* And with that, he felt a slight nip on his ear, the tickle of a frigid kiss, and he was released.

Light Stream plummeted. The cold villain floating above shrank rapidly, mockingly waving "bye-bye" as the hero fell. Light Stream struggled to regain flight, but he was falling too fast; the cold of that kiss clung to him like a memory.

That last night in the dorms. It was hot and humid. Both boys slept on top of their sheets, or tried to sleep. The sound of his roommate shifting restlessly above, struggling against the oppressive heat, was just too much. In his mind, he had climbed to the top bunk a thousand times and added his heat to that of his roommate. He noisily shifted on his mattress and in a moment of frustration stripped off his sweaty underwear and threw them into the middle of the room. Startled by his own rash action, he froze as his roommate moved heavily above. The mattress groaned, and he covered himself with the damp sheet as his roommate, too, tossed his underwear onto the floor. Both pairs overlapped—white flags of surrender on the threadbare carpet. Silence. Neither boy moved. And then from the top bunk, his roommate dangled one leg, then the other. An excruciating minute passed. The young Light Stream reached out and tentatively stroked one fuzzy calf. Both boys shivered, and in an instant, his roommate had jumped down and turned to face him, proudly displaying his body. His arms above his head, he gripped the railing of the bunk bed. Shadows leaked from his armpits and painted his rib cage and thin waist in darkness.

His roommate, who had always been so cold, never changing clothes when they were in the room together, now swayed alluringly just inches from his face. The young Light

Stream was breathless. Worried that he would accidentally levitate, he grabbed the mattress, and the sheet that covered his nakedness fell away. His roommate examined his body, first with his eyes, then with hesitant fingers. Both boys gasped as each simultaneously gripped the other's heat, sweaty palms demanding that they pull on one another and join, one boy on top the other, lips together, sharing the same hot breath yet never actually kissing except for a furtive nibble on his ear.

Falling fast as a bullet, Light Stream blinked. He must have momentarily passed out. With a burst of adrenaline, he summoned all of his power and braked *hard.* And the Ice King flew by as Light Stream hovered in midair to gain his bearings. The Ice King banked far below. Light Stream bobbed in the sky, the memories from college still fresh in his mind.

My roommate was always so cold.

Perplexed, Light Stream levitated and watched as the Ice King approached within a black cloud that trailed icy hail.

Impossible, he's so big. Well of course it could be him, why would I assume he'd still be so skinny? College was almost twenty years ago. Look at how I've changed.

And he realized he had changed in all the right ways.

No matter my challenges, I always faced them. My old roommate ran away. And look at what he has become.

❖

The Ice King drew on the knowledge of their first battle and surmised that Light Stream drew power from the sun. He kept the sky dark with thick snow clouds. Whenever the hero rallied, the Ice King would drop large formations of ice on the dumbstruck crowd shivering in the streets below, using Light

Stream's morality against him. Though the villain was proud of his strategy, and Light Stream certainly looked bested—blond hair matted to his back with frost and sweat—the Ice King couldn't help but feel the hero was holding back. He craved more than an epic melee and flew closer, to better encase his foe in ice and bring the combat to more intimate terms. The weary hero prepared for the onslaught and turned slightly so the Ice King would not see the ball of energy forming in his hand. But as he bobbed in the wind, he allowed the powerful globe of light to dissipate. He extended his hands, palms out, and tried another weapon.

The Ice King was upon him. Bitter cold lashed his cheeks as the villain raised his fists, now covered with frozen icicles, ready to pummel Light Stream.

"Kelvin, is that you?"

The Ice King faltered. The largest icicle protruding from his knuckles cracked and tumbled to the frozen waters below. No one had called him by his given name in years, not since he had gone cold at the laboratory. He'd thought that name was gone. Dead. Buried in the snowbanks of his fury.

"It's me, William, your roommate freshman year."

A variety of emotions flashed across the tundra of the Ice King's face. Reflexively, he fingered the scar on his arm. Light Stream floated closer and looked into the eyes of this killer, this madman, the dangerous freak who had playfully decimated the community Light Stream had sworn to protect. They had known each other briefly, during an innocent yet formative time, when neither knew what it was that they wanted, except that such desire made them outcasts. Light Stream's gaze was met with frosty resistance that wavered with recognition, and then longing.

They kissed. And Light Stream held the Ice King as the

surrounding storm cloud dissipated into harmless rain. His hapless former foe fumbled in the air and finally relented and clung to Light Stream, who continued to kiss him deeply, with a kiss of forgiveness, understanding, and passion. And it was too late for the wide-eyed villain to disengage once he realized that it was one of those rare kisses hot enough to melt ice.

Kid Cyclops

1973

The infant's disturbingly large, singular, and centered eye would have likely negated maternal instinct save its oceanic depth and the allure of serenity it offered to all that gazed into it. His mother cradled him gently and cooed and stroked the slick curlicue surprise of hair punctuating his broad forehead. She looked into the mirror of her son's wide-open eye. It reflected a glassy, twisted carnival image of her face, and she laughed. If she rejected this child, she would be the freak. If beauty was in the eye of the beholder, he was going to be one hell of a beholder. The baby blinked. Long lashes still damp with afterbirth struggled to disengage. She held him aloft, the better for him to see. She knew then that she would be his tripod and flagpole, that her efforts to hoist him up in a perilous world would bring him that much closer to the stars.

1974

Edwin dug his shovel into the sand and smoothed out the moat around the castle. The large bonnet his mother had strapped around his head bunched beneath his fleshy chin.

The sand castle didn't look right either. He struggled to stand, but his plump little legs still wavered under the weight of his massive cranium. He looked up and down the beach. A scattering of colorful umbrellas rolled toward the horizon like a dispersed rainbow. He could easily see for miles and took in the work of the other children. Some were capable diggers and had moats of note, but no minarets matched his. His mother was on her stomach on a towel, absorbed in a magazine. He wanted to pull on the skirt of her bathing suit and proudly show her the miniature spiral staircase fashioned from bits of shell that wound around the central tower, but he knew if he disturbed her, he would get another dab of noxious white cream on the nose. Unsatisfied, he searched the sand for driftwood to make a suitable drawbridge.

❖

The highchair was placed close enough to the kitchen table that between spoonfuls of applesauce delivered with exaggerated, sputtering airplane noises, he could read the newspaper propped up between his mother's plate and a wooden bowl of plump oranges. The article on the front page detailed how more and more Cyclops babies were being born.

As the next spoonful arrived, Edwin kicked his feet and shook his head from side to side and wailed. Concerned, his mother dropped the spoon on the tray and wiped the corner of his mouth, a perplexed look on her face. He pointed to the newspaper and asked, "Why didn't you tell me there were other babies like me?"

She swallowed, searched for composure, and found it. Taking up the spoon again, she fed herself a dollop of applesauce and looked him in the eye. A series of complex emotions crossed her face: pride, deep worry, fear, even amusement. Amusement won, and with a wry cock of her head, she finally replied, "Well, Edwin, I didn't know you could talk, so I didn't tell you. Now why don't you tell me when you learned to read?"

She held a spoonful of applesauce tauntingly before him, this time minus the sound of flight.

1975

Because it was deemed important to science, but mostly because he wanted to, Edwin was placed in a room with another baby Cyclops. His previous exposure to other children had been somewhat limited. Other babies liked him and smiled when caught in the gaze of the clear and compelling opal clasped between his tiny, upturned nose and immense forehead. It was the parents that balked, that pulled their children away or picked up speed when their strollers happened to pass. Sure, his mother had a few open-minded friends that would schedule a play date. He rolled with it but ultimately preferred his mother's company, the feel of her flesh and her ready laugh and protecting hands. When she was busy, he relished listening to NPR, then relatively new. Television was a nuisance; the four stations spewed too many colors without respect to one another. Never mind the narratives and noise. Edwin would prefer staring at a William Turner painting for hours over television any day of the week.

The room was sterile and obvious, the clinically casual display of Lincoln Logs and colorful toys obviously meant to test social interactive skills and intelligence. The two-way mirror was a joke, but he went along with it, hating that his mother had dressed up and even worn lipstick, giving the unseen scientists more respect than he felt they deserved. A door opened and a haggard woman with thinning hair walked in, holding her own Cyclops baby at arm's length. She placed the child gently on the floor, stared at the two-way mirror, and then fled, not even looking at Edwin or his mother, who smiled at him and followed the distraught woman out.

The other Cyclops baby was necessarily younger. Edwin had been the first, which was a point of pride. He was thrilled to read his name in *The Wall Street Journal*, which he had pressed his mother to subscribe to. He didn't agree with their politics, but he only read the *Times* on Sunday, and the *Journal* had great font and nifty illustrations. Still, none of the articles had mentioned that any of the Cyclops babies, including him, could talk or read; only that it was a global phenomenon of small but growing proportions. This had left him and his mother to wonder if he was alone in his abilities or if the other parents were covering out of concern.

The other child eagerly crawled toward him full tilt, grinning and drooling to an extent that Edwin's anticipation flagged. Then the child touched him with a painter's touch, a soft, reading caress of his face. And of course the eye told the whole story, its openness like a summer lake, Edwin fell into the other infant's eye and swam about in the universal mystery that was and will always be the present. Both felt an electrical charge ignite within their corneas. Too excited to obey caution, Edwin broke away from the fraternal gaze of the other Cyclops baby and spoke directly to the two-way mirror.

"Hey, Mom, tell them to turn off the lights."

He returned to the other infant. They playfully interlaced thick fingers and gurgled with delight as a silent but surely intense argument took place behind the mirror. He knew Mom would make her presence felt, that she had finished her requisite task of counseling the poor wreck that birthed his new comrade and was ready to run the show backstage. Sure enough, the lights went off, save the single red light of a video camera barely perceptible behind the thick glass.

The babies tightened their grip on one another and chortled as they blinked, and intense beams of blue light shot out their particular eyes. Strong light, light that could shine for miles, as powerful as any movie premiere spotlight. Both children knew not to look at the glass mirror, as their illumination was strong enough to blind anyone on the other side. Even with the thickness of the glass, Edwin heard someone hit the floor, having fainted. But he knew it wasn't his mother, that she was nodding her head to no one in particular, eyes narrowed, elated to have birthed a new source of light.

1987

In high school, he was expected to play defense. All male teenage Cyclopes succumbed to this role, and though he was more interested in being on the debate team, he had to accept whatever level of acceptance was offered. Edwin wondered if the other Cyclopes *liked* football. The strategy didn't rise to the level of chess, though he did find the camaraderie and the jokes fun. The baseball players seemed smarter, but the school was centered on football.

The steam of the shower room clung to him like a weather system. Big for his age, the bathroom at home was so confining that he looked forward to showering at school. The other boys didn't dare tease him about his central eye. His strength on the field was apparent, as was his intelligence in the classroom. The blond hair that had swirled around his head as an infant had receded. When puberty set in, pubic hair and underarm hair did not follow. His legs and arms were hairless, though fortunately everything else grew in stature as his height surpassed that of his classmates. No one joked with him about his size, his lack of hair, or his one probing eye. The other kids were nice but intimidated.

No other Cyclopes lived in his hometown. Two were close by in the nearest city; he chatted with them on the phone. Twins, both were really into languages and spoke over a dozen fluently. Though that wasn't Edwin's forte, he enjoyed their enthusiasm and had even agreed to join them on an upcoming field trip to the UN. All they talked about on the phone was what school they wanted to get into and what career paths genuinely suited this new minority that, whenever together, could slice the sky with arctic blue swords of light.

Toweling off, Edwin thought less about the twins and what they would chat about for hours that evening, and more about one of his teammates. Diego had followed him out of the showers. Of Edwin's fellow athletes, Diego alone lingered after practice and engaged him in meaningful conversation. Some of it inadvertently helped Diego with his homework, but his interest seemed to go beyond typical football banter and toward something neither of them could define, yet both enjoyed.

Diego chatted amiably, naked, holding his underwear in his hands, forever about to don them but never quite taking that necessary step. His hair was impossibly black and thick. What little equally dark hair marched down his chest resembled the curly mass that bunched at his crotch. His body was naturally strong, his muscles classically articulated. His every move, his every action on and off the field, seemed effortless and right. It was all Edwin could do to fight off an erection. Rudely, he turned his back to Diego and was simply dismissive.

"Okay, D., I'll see you later."

Unbothered, Diego finally stepped into his underwear and shorts and replied, "Sure thing, Eddie, see you tomorrow."

The other boy walked back to his own locker, never imagining the red anguish that welled within his friend's massive orb.

1988

Junior year, Edwin stayed home. He tested out, graduated early, and spent his days doing push-ups in the backyard, listening to NPR, and worrying about the future. No one had guessed they'd get *this* big. He couldn't fit into a car anymore, and even if he wanted to go somewhere, his size was so imposing that people literally screamed when they saw him. Fortunately his mother had made an anticipatory move and used her new career as a real estate agent to trade their confining two-bedroom home for something much larger. It was out in the country, surrounded by cow fields, with a swimming pool he could lounge in and a carport he could sleep under. Though still new, the Internet was used primarily by the US government, but it was assumed that this would be a good way for the Cyclopes to communicate since they had grown too large to use phones or write letters. A new company, Apple Computers, had designed state-of-the-art giant cloth keypads to go along with their new personal computers and donated sets of them to the entire Cyclops brethren. When he wasn't chatting with the twins about the injustice of the Cyclops ban at the Olympics, he eagerly awaited Diego's visits.

Diego was the only teammate who stopped by after class or on the weekends. Living out in the country as well, it was natural for him to come over and swim on hot summer days. He brought gossip from the school, none of which interested Edwin much. Best were their silent moments under the sun, when the heat relaxed Edwin enough to the point where he could actually imagine reaching out to the other teen and holding his hand.

But Diego had lately talked about girls, so Edwin had worked hard to banish the burgeoning fantasies and enjoy the simple company of his fellow athlete. One morning, Diego showed up earlier than usual and surprised Edwin in the backyard. The young Cyclops was now so enormous he bathed in the sturdy aboveground pool. Never shy, Edwin usually wore just a pair of special Lycra shorts that stretched with his body, what Diego had teasingly called his "Hulk pants," but his friend now caught him naked, comically scrubbing his back with a sudsy push broom. Diego came jogging around the corner, shirt over one shoulder, and said, "Let me give you a hand."

Before a red-faced Edwin could say anything, Diego kicked off natty sneakers, jumped up onto the diving board, and beckoned for the broom. Edwin sheepishly turned it over and relaxed his shoulders, letting the football player get to work. Having someone else scrub him was immensely relaxing, and he eased down into the pool and unlocked his knees. He closed his lone eye and relinquished the burden of fear. The sky was a cloudless blue, the summer heat was not yet unbearable, and his mom was showing a house on the other side of town.

Diego took his time, joking that he'd gained the necessary experience washing school buses for detention. Edwin finally just let it happen: he was tired of turning his back on desire, on his friend. Legs spread, his considerable erection struggled to its full length. It popped out of the water like a pink porpoise, and in the impending wake, Diego whistled. With the previously unheard rasp of awe in his voice, he whispered, "I've wondered what it looked like now."

He dropped the broom and circled the pool. Edwin raised his buttocks ever so slightly and sighed. Exposed, it felt like

Krakatoa, a new island emerging from the sea, volcanic flesh begging to be explored. Diego stripped off his cargo shorts and underwear and grabbed a beach towel. He gave an enthusiastic shout and plunged into the water between the Cyclops's legs. He surfaced and wiped the water off his face. Steadying himself with one hand on the wide column of Edwin's ankle, he announced, "I'm going to give you a scrubbing like you've never had before!"

Edwin relaxed farther into the water, the apprehension that had normally twisted his stomach whenever he and Diego were naked together in the locker room replaced by a more welcoming heat that spread throughout his body. Diego worked in earnest, robustly applying the now-soaked towel between the Cyclops's toes. The palm of Diego's hand on any part of his body was like an electric shock. When the athlete pressed his own robust erection against Edwin's skin, it was like the strike of a match. But none of the half-formed thoughts that tantalized Edwin at night materialized into anything now that Diego was present and apparently willing. His formidable erection flagged. Diego took note and let the soaked towel float away.

"Losing interest, eh?"

Before Edwin could protest, Diego scrambled up the giant's knee, his hands and feet digging into his flesh, giving Edwin another round of goose bumps. Panting, Diego stood still on Edwin's knee and let his friend examine his perfect body, the shock of his tan line, the elliptical bulge of his thighs. Edwin's confidence, and quite a bit more, was restored.

Under the spotlight of his friend's single, probing eye, Diego whispered, "Lift me up."

The Cyclops blinked, swallowed, and obeyed. Holding Diego aloft, he felt the same sensations as when he masturbated. The flesh in his hand was hard, masculine, and more important, it *belonged* to him. Diego sighed, and Edwin panicked at the thought he might be crushing his friend and released him into the water with a splash. Diego surfaced with a laugh. He shook the water out of his hair and paddled close to the base of the Cyclops's erection. Beneath the water, Edwin's testicles undulated like large jellyfish. But Diego was an explorer and put his hands everywhere, touching every nook and cranny of flesh. When he wasn't using his hands, he used his mouth to climb a living mountain of a man, and when they both reached the peak, two friends became lovers and the summer heat finally seeped into their bones and painted their skin with well-deserved sweat.

1990

Somewhere behind the line of camouflaged Cyclopes, giant speakers in the back of a jeep pumped out AC/DC to rattle the enemy and pump up the troops. Edwin held hands with the twins, and they and their fellow giants blasted the approaching Iraqi tanks in unison with their eyebeams. Munitions within the tanks exploded, ripping through metal carriages turned molten orange. The tanks rolled to a stop and became a mass of sputtering flame in a matter of seconds. Scorched sand cratered. Overhead, helicopters prepared to deposit troops behind the slowly advancing wall of Cyclopes. Broken twists of oil wells burned in the distance, staining the sky an insolent inky black. Up and down the line, beams of light seared the now decimated Iraqi army. The Cyclopes had been on Kuwaiti soil for less than hour, and the invasion was routed.

Edwin closed his eye and pulled the light and the heat

back into the recesses of his powerful orb. If he unclasped hands with the twins, their light would recede, a dangerous move even though the fighting seemed to be over. At the far end of the line, he heard the sound of a grenade and responding gunfire, and he felt the weight of his compatriots pull in that direction. Whistles were blown, signaling that they could let go. He sensed the tension and understood: one of his fellow Cyclopes must have been hit. Several of his comrades broke into a run, but he and the exhausted twins slumped to the ground.

With his considerable vision, he was able to see a bloody leg twisted the wrong way through the distant smoke. A perplexed medic stood beside a severed finger the size of a typical human body. This was Edwin's worst fear realized. No matter the planning, their unique size made the Cyclopes susceptible to injury and difficult to treat. And most were here. Every Cyclops in the world had been offered citizenship and scholarships galore to the American university of their choice should they serve two years in the Marines.

The majority accepted, save those few from Communist countries who'd been kept apart from their Cyclops compatriots and brainwashed into militaristic state property. These were the minority, as most of their brethren were born below a certain parallel in the warmer regions of the earth. Still, enough Russian Cyclopes existed to have gained the Soviet Empire a new lease on life, which, in turn, frightened enough Americans into altering the Constitution, lending Reagan yet another landslide re-election, this time for his third and, he swore, final term.

Edwin rubbed his own aching forehead as one of the twins eagerly massaged his shoulders. Whenever the Cyclopes were together, they compulsively and repeatedly touched one another as if starved for affection. So far, every single Cyclops he had met or communicated with was solely attracted to other Cyclopes of the same sex. Back in the circus tent of their makeshift barracks, they whispered among each other about pairing with opposite-sex Cyclopes to continue "their race," which in turn led to a raucous debate over whether they were a separate species or if evolution had taken a new direction and then changed its mind. No new Cyclops had been born in over a decade. Yet after lights out, all Edwin could think about was Diego, who had impulsively joined the Army when Edwin enlisted. Edwin had tried to explain his reasons for enlisting were far from patriotic. This was a life-changing opportunity for Cyclopes to gather and decide on their purpose as a group plus pay for college—something of huge significance, as many of their families were going broke keeping them fed. When Congress lowered the age of enlistment to sixteen, however, the entire football team signed up for the Army, and his brash lover didn't understand that even though they would be fighting in the same war together, they might not ever see each other, *be* together.

Another large contingent of helicopters menaced the sky. With the war likely already over, Edwin was hopeful Diego was safe, but overall he was more worried than relieved. *Will this rekindle Reagan's obsession with Central America?* The fine print of their enlistment papers allowed for reactivation for specific yet ill-defined threats. They had all been assured they were needed for Iraq. Now he wasn't so sure.

Distant gunfire faded. Jets silently carved the sky above. Whoever manned the jeep with the giant speakers either had a sick sense of humor or a prescient understanding of American history. At a slightly lower volume, "We've Only Just Begun," by the Carpenters, caressed the desert sand.

1998

The ceremony was appropriately solemn and only slightly awkward. It was over much too quickly to warrant such a gathering of power and dignitaries. Everyone shuffled about and were then ushered back into place as it was re-enacted for different camera angles. The heroes had cool costumes while Edwin had to make do with his typical gray camouflage. He noticed the other heroes winced or turned ever so slightly from the repetitive bursts of flashbulbs, but Edwin never wavered. Capes swirled and bored mutants moaned, ready for the buffet laid out at the reception in the underground bunker. The World Guardians had been following his story in the newspapers since he was a baby, just as he knew of them, more or less, from the comic book retelling of their adventures and the badly made TV movies. Several made sure they gave him private words of encouragement. One hero, Light Stream, kindly offered to take him camping up in Canada, describing a snowy desolation that warmed the Cyclops's soul.

To the military and the World Guardians' chagrin, he couldn't fit through the bunker's entrance and was spared the uncomfortable small talk that always accompanied such events. He strolled along the shore of Governor's Island, ostensibly his new home, though he longed for isolation and hoped that Light Stream's offer was sincere. His last home, the USS *Colin Powell*, was moored nearby. The towers of Manhattan loomed just beyond the aircraft carrier, each equally gray in the light rain, and each too populated for him to easily bear. Construction equipment was strewn about the freshly laid airstrip—the island was being prepped to house the heroes' headquarters. A rusted World War Two–era aircraft hangar had been retrofitted to serve as his abode for the time being.

He was twenty-five and a veteran of two wars, one for the greater good, one ill-conceived and poorly executed. He'd left too many brothers and sisters buried in the jungles of Honduras and quietly wished Diego had been killed in action as well. Edwin's star status in the Gulf War had allotted him power he was willing to wield for the benefit of his Cyclops crew, gaining them better protective gear and improved medical treatment. With extreme difficulty, he even managed the reassignment of Diego to the Marines as his personal attaché. As the war in Nicaragua widened, the once-formidable Cyclops troops were stretched thin. Urban combat decimated their numbers, and the jungles were even worse. Determined and trained Communist guerillas made for more recalcitrant foes than the reluctant Iraqi Army. Diego was prepared to do anything to serve his now high-ranking lover, but the tense, often deeply intellectual and strategic conversation among the Cyclopes often alienated him. The other enlisted men guessed his liaison with Edwin, so he faced ostracism on that front. Edwin had tried desperately to salvage the relationship. Rest and relaxation in Aruba provided brief, naked moments in the green surf. But for Diego, with blood and bombs came the bottle.

The noble band of Cyclopes fared far worse. The surviving twin was a professional wrestler addicted to crystal meth who spastically hit on him whenever they ran into each other. At least he could stand. The few others who remained were in wheelchairs at prestigious universities, for with their impressive size came insidious blood clots that either killed or crippled. Where men his age had acne scars, Edwin had bullet wounds and buried comrades. Though the Guardians had bestowed upon him the moniker "Kid Cyclops," he felt like anything but.

The rain let up but the sky darkened, threatening more inclement weather. This was his first night as an official member of the World Guardians. He knew he had been offered a role with the team less as a consolation prize and more as a way to ease him out of military life. After all, homosexuality was reason for dismissal, and without a war to obscure it, better a quick, "heroic" exit.

Edwin stopped at a small jetty facing the Statue of Liberty. From what his mother and Diego's parents had gathered, Diego had been arrested for public intoxication in Manhattan just a few months ago and was still likely there, living off various charities and aid from the Veterans Administration. They knew he was homeless and Edwin thought it was ironic they would end up so close together, yet separated by far more than a river. His love for Diego had set him apart from the other Cyclopes. Now that he was among the last, it was still a bit of a shock that his powers worked without the touch of another of his kind. Wistfully, he hoped this came from his time with Diego, and that he would have something like that again with another. It was time to rejoin the party. Really, though, he just wanted to listen to NPR.

That morning, the radio incredulously reported that several dogs, all different but large breeds in multiple countries only in the southern hemisphere, had all died while giving birth to similar mutations with striking gold beaks and brown feathers. Though the commentators had yet to name them, Edwin had. He was quite curious to see how soon, after shaking off the afterbirth and finding proper footing, the wings on these coltish Griffins would set them aloft, to sing through challenging though nonetheless expansive skies.

Mutinous Chocolate

The box of chocolates rested on the nightstand like a casket at some banal wake, its dark, foiled contents blandly necessary to the room. To throw the box away would lessen Rich's fury toward Alex; the sudden absence of this poisonous gift would be more dramatic than its presence. Worse, he was now of an age where he understood the intrinsic mechanisms of a breakup but as yet could not lessen the impact. He had chosen to ignore certain signs, and after it had come to a head, he had mistakenly allowed the final conversation to be held over red wine at a new restaurant he had read about and wanted to try. But they didn't get around to ordering more than a bottle of Cabernet, salads, and a skimpy appetizer each.

Alex had offered to dissolve their several-months-old relationship as if it were something on the menu considered and discarded. Rich had made the fatal mistake of all such dissolutions delivered in conversational tones by acting as if said blandishments, since calmly stated, were debatable. Counteroffers were made and rebuffed over small shreds of arugula. And more wine, Alex conspicuously filling Rich's glass to the brim while conservatively sipping his own half-filled Crate & Barrel goblet. Always that self-assured smile on his face, chin up, his eyes half-closed to better accentuate the serenity he wished to project, emphasizing the long lashes that drove Rich to distraction.

Back at Rich's apartment, the sex was perfunctory. Alex was slow and rhythmic where he had always been harsh and taunting in bed, beguiling with a hint of brutality. Now he was annoyingly kind, as if afraid to hurt his now ex-lover further. *If this is good-bye, then good-bye already*, Rich thought, his knees pushing into his smooth dark chest as Alex cooed above him in Spanish. *I want a man in my bed, not someone from the Visiting Nurse Service!* Rich thought. Alex closed his eyes as he came. Rich lay there, hands behind his shaved head braced for more, but he knew he couldn't have an orgasm. He grabbed a Kleenex from the box beside the bed and quickly pretended to mop up a nonexistent spill from his hard, rippled stomach. His extinguished former lover rolled to one side and presented his beautiful back to Rich, whose sadness intensified as the singular freckles and thick moles that shimmied across Alex's broad shoulders and whittled down his spine now seemed as out of reach as the unseen stars outside.

Still drunk, Rich fumbled across the prone and sleeping form beside him and turned off the light. He wanted to cry himself asleep, cry loud enough for Alex to wake up, truly wake up and realize his mistake so they could hold each other forever. The tears did not come, and his sorrow was replaced by the kind of anger that would eventually metastasize within the nurturing darkness of an intense hangover to hatch ridiculous revenge scenarios and horrific one-night stands. Emotionally exhausted, Rich finally fell asleep, curious rather than bitter as to where the morning's pain would lead.

Rude light raked the room. He rose and irritably pulled the curtains shut, then leaned against them to feel the coldness of the glass leech through the fabric and dull the pain in his forehead. Enough light seeped in that he could tell it was past noon. Before he turned around, he knew that the bed would be empty, a disastrous ruin of rumpled sheet and sweat-soaked pillows. He would have to call in sick. It was too late to go into work, and worse, he would have to do laundry. Alex had left him, and now he would have to go to the basement laundry room and wash the man's smells from his sheets. The bits of him that salted the pillow could be rinsed away, but it would take more wine and many, many nights to get him out of his mind.

Rich's apartment was a studio on a high floor, well-appointed with compact furniture from the MOMA store and Design Within Reach. Alex had quietly left that morning, presumably returning to his dingy Elmhurst apartment, a drafty walkup with a landlady who loudly mocked him in a thick Hungarian accent that he never brought home any girls. Rich parted the curtain and looked out at the gray steam twisting off a myriad of Manhattan rooftops. Central Park peeked from behind a cluster of grand monuments. *He left this for that? My doorman knew his name by his third visit!*

He rolled himself in the curtain and the light rushed back in, illuminating a heart-shaped box on the nightstand. A box of chocolates, meant as a parting gift but really a reminder that something even more sweet was gone, a box filled with bitter emptiness, replete with venomous coils of lacy ribbon. No card. None needed. After all, Alex had said good-bye, and Alex always meant what he said. An intense fury welled up within him, and he lunged across the bed and batted the package to the floor, where it landed softly within the folds of the white faux-fur rug. He rolled off the bed and stepped into his silk boxers, pulled them up roughly, and marched toward the kitchen. The refrigerator was empty save an old orange and a bottle of champagne. He reached for the bottle and decided it was time to break in one of the Baccarat flutes he'd bought years ago, having secretly savored the idea that he would keep them in reserve for an engagement yet to come.

It didn't take long to polish off the bottle of champagne. Daytime television churned pretty colors on the mounted flat screen, which consumed most of the wall opposite the bed. He'd already jettisoned the planned excursion to the laundry room and instead stared at the television. The sound was off, the figures on the screen bleached faceless by the constant sun. He had found a bottle of rum under the sink and ordered Chinese, which remained untouched on the counter by the stove, though the two Diet Cokes he'd also ordered were gone, as was the rum.

Time had slowed, and the room was comfortable, finite. Nothing was outside but pain and disappointment, and that was why the door was locked and his phone was off. Rich was curled up on the floor, wrapped in a raggedy bathrobe from his college years. Half of the rug clung to his legs. He was hungry but unable to differentiate his animal needs from his emotional wants, so he reached for the half-drunk glass of rum and Diet Coke, now watery from melted ice. The glass was nowhere near him; it rested on the white Ikea table in the breakfast nook—he'd have to stand up to get it. Crossing the room was beyond him. Dejected, he let his arm fall heavily at his side, nearly denting the discarded red box of rueful candy. Assuming that some of the chocolates likely had a liquor filling, he tore at the ribbons and pulled off the lid.

The alcohol and disappointment that clouded his mind rapidly receded as he examined the inlay of meticulously parceled morsels. Each shone like a jewel; a variety of colorfully foiled truffles crowded a bed of lush red velvet. Suddenly he was ravenous and wanted to tear into the box, devour this last vestige of Alex, but the singularity of each piece gave him pause. These were not your typical drugstore-

Saran-wrapped-I'm-sorry-I-gave-you-an-STD-chocolates. He looked at the back of the lid, but it didn't offer a diagram of the contents. *Classy. This is the real deal, probably from one of those little boutiques on the East Side.* He plucked a candy from the middle of the box. The scent of a distant cinnamon filled the air, as if a faraway galleon had gone down in a storm, and its fractured freight had washed ashore. Rich closed his eyes to better savor the smell. A strong tangerine lurked beneath the cinnamon, dark, bitter, heavy, muddled and fermented, a potion, a teaspoon of which would numb restless children into a dreamless sleep. A drop in a doorway would ward off black widow spiders. He sat up, alert to the treasure in his palm as well as subdued and seduced by its fragrance.

Gingerly, he unfolded the thick, metallic wrapping. Cinnamon powder flecked his fingertips. Parched, he craved a glass of water to cleanse his palate, to truly deserve the sacrament he was about to put in his mouth. *This piece of Alex.* He stood unsteadily, his knees shaking. He was unsure if he should part from the chocolate for even a moment, fraught with the anxiety that comes with trivial indecision. The light coming through the wall-length window was a dazzling orange, nearly gold. The sun was about to set. His first day without Alex was coming to a close. He *deserved* chocolate. Without further hesitation, Rich bit into the truffle. The richness was not startling; he expected something so meticulously dressed to live up to its packaging. That it was so good was almost a letdown. *Predictably divine.* He popped the rest of the truffle between his lips and stepped toward the bathroom.

An orchard of sun-warmed tangerines blossomed in his mouth, heavy, overly ripe tangerines that hung perilously from trees dark with leaves of the blackest mint.

Rich fell to his knees and grasped at the shag rug. Wide-eyed, he felt storm clouds gathering at the back of his throat, dark shadows that enveloped the grove. A bittersweet chocolate rain fell. Black raindrops hit the earth heavily in cinnamon explosions, and he rolled onto his side and cried for the love he lost when Alex went out the door.

At midnight, he rose and went into the bathroom to draw a bath. As the tub filled, he drank from the sink. Rather than feeling hungover or famished, Rich felt both relaxed and ready. He craved the bath more to wash away the stain of the breakup rather than settle any frayed nerves. As far as he was concerned, the night had only just begun. After his bath, he was going out and didn't plan on coming home alone. An aqueous cloud of lavender-tinted bubbles beckoned. But after shimmying out of his boxers, he turned off the tap and went back into the living room. The box of chocolates sat benignly on the floor. He picked it up and examined it. He couldn't see a barcode, nothing to connote which store it had come from. He scanned the nightstand for the thousandth time. No card. He quickly stripped the sheets from the bed and placed the chocolates in the center of the mattress, a red pearl on the cotton tongue of a queen-sized jewelry box. Rich turned and dramatically skipped toward the rising heat of the waiting bath.

❖

The late night crowd at Stag Bar was predictably desperate, high, drunk, touristy, and available. It had been several months since Rich had gone cruising, and he loved it. It was like shopping in a foreign city he knew well yet infrequently visited. He wanted to kiss many men, grope several crotches—select just the right lay to put his shattered relationship behind him. In the basement bar, he ordered a Long Island Iced Tea with no intent on pacing himself. He quickly drank it and ordered another. Having just been tipped a twenty, the bartender was as attentive as a surgeon and looked genuinely concerned when Rich moved away to approach a young Hispanic man with a huge diamond earring and an immaculately sculpted beard. *Too much like Alex. I need to replace him entirely. No reruns tonight, honey.* He abruptly swept past the youth, who cocked an annoyed eyebrow and turned to reengage the fat white guy in a rumpled business suit who had desperately but incoherently been trying to pick him up.

Upstairs, the lights pulsed with the music. Boys swayed together or alone with their drinks. He finished his drink and deposited the glass on the tray of a passing waiter, shirtless in tight cut-off jean shorts, pale chest waxen beneath the revolving lights, wispy blond hair hung over flawless features and mascara-inflected dead eyes. Another model-actor-singer mildly surprised he wasn't an overnight success in the big city. Shock replaced by bitterness after multiple degrading episodes. Meaningless gigs and supposedly career-advancing blow jobs that lead to the realization that he was but one of a multitude of pretty boys competing to fill a *single* pair of underwear in a Times Square billboard.

Rich pushed through the crowd. *And there's the perfect candidate*, he thought, spying a ridiculously tall young man on the dance floor. Tattoos poured down his upraised ebony arms. He had the ugly nose of someone who had been in a few fights, and his sharp, well-groomed eyebrows accented an intelligent face. The boy parted thick lips to flick a pierced tongue at Rich. The song changed and gave them a new rhythm with which to find each other, and Rich placed his large hands on the boy's lissome hips, quickly confirming the boy wasn't wearing any underwear.

His jeans hung well below a belly button shrouded in perfect swirls of hair leading to a mammoth knot within the folds of his True Religion jeans. Rich lifted the boy's polo shirt as the boy stroked his own nipples—fingers long and spidery with blunt tips and perfect shiny nails. They danced closer and kissed. The boy tasted like a fresh mint disguising an invisible, growing hunger, something feral. Rich leaned in as if to kiss him again but instead dove toward one of his armpits and sniffed deeply: a mammal scent barely masked by cheap, dissipating deodorant. He put the boy's hand on his own rock-hard crotch. The young man laughed, obviously pleased with the treasure in his grasp and announced in a deep, richly smooth voice, "We're going. I don't know where, but we are definitely *going*."

"My place, let's catch a cab," Rich replied, taking him by the hand. They marched toward the exit.

They made out in the back of the cab, the bored Sikh driver ignoring them while talking on his cell phone for the duration of the short ride uptown. Rich stopped at the liquor store for vodka and wine, then a bodega for limes and assorted groceries while his date rapidly smoked a menthol outside, rocking expectantly back and forth on his heels. They silently looked into each other's eyes on the elevator ride up—the boy trying out different, slightly comic seductive looks, and Rich deciding that he wanted to be the top tonight to get the aggression out of his system. Curious about the surprises in store for him, he pushed the door to his apartment open and flung the groceries on the counter as he turned to watch the boy undress.

"I'm Tony, by the way." Suddenly shy, he turned his back to Rich while he stepped out of his jeans.

"You told me in the cab. Leave your shirt on while I fix us drinks." Rich exhaled and went about cutting up lemons for some stiff vodka tonics. He scooped some crushed ice out of the freezer and flung the shards into the full glasses, splashing alcohol all over the kitchen counter. He pictured Tony on his back on his bed, legs parted and knees bent, an erection wavering above the folds of his stomach. He loved it when a man was naked from the waist down; something about partial covering turned him on. This reversal was intrinsically erotic to him, like how you normally see a man without a shirt on the beach or in the park, but never the opposite. He turned toward the bed, and his mouth dropped. Tony was on his stomach, revealing a smooth, amazingly humpy butt and long, strong, practically hairless legs. Bare feet playfully bounced off his pillows.

The box of chocolates was open—Tony had a dark cylindrical piece balanced between his large, perfect teeth. Rich almost dropped the drinks to lunge at the boy and snatch it out of his mouth, but his naturally calculating curiosity took over. He took a long drink of vodka and bent down before the expectant boy.

"Go ahead, take a bite." He squatted now and clinically observed as Tony exaggeratedly bit down on the chocolate in his mouth, sealing his lips with a smile and running a tongue over his lips.

"Mmm. Cherry." The boy closed his eyes and seemed momentarily in a trance.

He shook himself out of it and regarded Rich with a daring look. Rich quickly finished his drink and set the boy's on the floor. He pulled his shirt over his head and unbuckled his belt as Tony animatedly flipped on his back and smiled widely, intoxicated, mouth open, ready to be kissed. Rich stepped out of his pants and pulled his underwear down to his ankles and kicked them off. He stepped onto the bed and fell over Tony. Their erections brushed as Rich went straight for his mouth, hands firmly clasping the boy's head, gently forcing his jaw open so he could mine the remnants of the chocolate from his tongue.

Their kiss was dark and rich and tasted of faraway fruit, cold in a moonless midnight orchard. He let the boy go and rolled onto his side as a soft red glow enveloped him. Eyeing Rich's impressive cock, the boy opened his mouth to reveal a red, pointed tongue. As he bent over to lick Rich's dick, Rich almost recoiled but was mesmerized by the electric horns emerging from Tony's scalp. They sparked every time Tony blinked his now pink, reptilian eyes. The scent of cherries with just a foggy hint of chocolate pervaded the apartment. The boy glowed as he writhed and twisted on Rich's cock, his long fingers digging into his thighs. Rich cupped the youth's ample ass and was surprised when a long and slender tail wrapped around his wrist, pulling him toward the boy's wanton hole. So coaxed, he stroked and played with Tony's ass as the boy continued to worship his cock. Rich was amazed at this new tail. Each time he penetrated Tony's ass with a fingertip, the appendage would stiffen and tighten its grip.

With his other hand, he reached beneath Tony and pulled on the hard flesh that swung between his parted legs. The boy moaned and disengaged from Rich's cock to wag his own formidable weapon back at him. Rich dove down and tasted sweet pre-cum. The cherry taste tingled on his tongue, and he pushed the boy backward and held his legs apart, feet now hoofed, black and shiny. The tail unwound from his arm and, as Rich tenderly probed the boy's rear with his hungry tongue, it wavered in the air, vibrating in tandem to his every thrust and lick.

Neither could wait any longer. Rich reached behind him and felt around on the floor until he located the forgotten vodka and tonic. He fished some splinters of ice from the drink and plunged them into the boy's anticipatory opening. Tony growled as Rich then slathered his cock with spit and vodka and placed the tip at the moist opening before him. He plunged inward and pushed the boy's legs farther apart. They were both now completely enveloped in a throbbing halo of crimson light. Their sweat was tinged black with enticing chocolate. They licked each other and themselves madly as they fucked. Rich didn't even bother to pull out as he came. Injecting his hot fluid into the boy, he bent over at an impossible angle to catch Tony's orgasm in his wide-open mouth. Gob after gob of hot and deliciously sweet cherry cream poured down his throat as the boy whimpered and thrashed beneath him.

Momentarily relenting, his still-stiff cock nestled within the contracting warm beneath him, Rich wiped chocolate sweat from his forehead and fed the nectar to the boy from his fingertips. Disoriented, Tony licked Rich's fingertips, his eyes oscillating like two hummingbirds.

The spell was broken—the red glow faded and was gone. Tony was overcome, nervous that Rich had not pulled out, unsure of what had just happened.

"I guess I make strong drinks," Rich had offered weakly as the boy quickly dressed, looking from the still-full vodka and tonic on the floor and back to Rich. He rushed to the bathroom, washed his face, and was out the door.

Rich turned off the lights and opened the curtains and settled back onto the damp mattress. The innumerable lights of the city shone as always, reaching out to him to let him know he was never alone.

❖

He was obligated to show his face at work, but not necessarily to do a good job. Putting recent events out of his mind, he plowed through a ridiculous number of emails, constantly checking his cell to see if Alex had called or sent a text message. He made a show of ordering in chicken soup to support his having previously called out sick, and left early. Instead of going home, he went to the gym, where he tried to work out the returning frustrations of Alex. *Should I have asked him to move in? My place was obviously too small, and every time he complained about his apartment I ignored him, thinking he was fishing for an invitation...I should have at least said we could get a place together, not Queens of course, but one-bedrooms are still halfway affordable uptown...*

He stepped off the treadmill and headed toward the showers, disgusted he couldn't excise these thoughts from his head. In the steam room, he noticed a few of the manly shapes were fit and tall and out of habit settled near them. Within the obliterating gray clouds of steam, he opened his towel and relaxed. Images from the night before, of Tony's body, flipped through his mind like random pages of a magazine. He remembered Tony's supple, hairless ass and his cock stirred. He opened his eyes to see if anyone else in the steam room was jacking off. The shapes were too indistinct. At least no one was chatting about stocks and sports. He wiped sweat from his forehead and spread his legs wider, recalling Tony opening his red, glowing devil eyes with serpentine slits the shade of bright, new vagina pink. He sat up as his hard-on deflated, then he pulled his towel tight and headed out to his locker.

Lost in dark thoughts, he barely noticed a young man had followed him out of the steam room. Toweling absentmindedly before his locker, he eventually noticed someone was checking him out. A diminutive, muscular guy still in his underwear had left his shirt open and was definitely trying to catch his eye. Short, white, corporate. The opposite of Alex. Rich let his towel drop and smiled his biggest smile, the one that said *I'm the catch of the day*. The young man at the other end of the aisle at first turned away. He quickly regained his composure, though, and turned back to exhibit an endearing blush plus half of a plump erection proudly filling fresh black Jockeys. Rich nodded approvingly and jerked his head toward the door, then quickly got dressed.

When they met outside and introduced themselves, Rich was pleased the boy was as eager as he was young, but not so eager that he didn't mind skipping a cab. Rich wanted to walk home, feel the city, and give this pretty little imp a chance to fall for him. He let him do most of the talking, but whenever they crossed the street, Rich would hold his hand as if he were a child or they were long-term, carefree lovers, testing him to see if he were a closet case or up for anything. Each time, the boy gladly accepted his hand and, in turn, squeezed Rich's hand *hard*. Rich liked that; this guy was letting know he that he was on to him and had the strength to take it.

Well, I always liked a little pain. He laughed out loud at his private joke and flashed a smile at his impromptu date. The guy smiled back at him, and Rich was glad they were in front of his building. He looked down at his crotch and thrust it forward slightly, so the boy could see his erection against his pants leg. The young man stepped past him, close, letting his knuckles brush against Rich's clothed cock. Rich shuddered at such a brazen, public move and followed him into the lobby.

The elevator was crowded, but this didn't stop the young man from swinging a hand backward to graze Rich's now fully erect penis every time someone got on or off the car.

Once inside, however, his cock lost some of its tumescence upon seeing the young man's barely disguised reaction to his apartment. Usually tricks were impressed, but this guy hesitated at the door as Rich rushed to open the curtains to distract from the mess that had become his home.

"Um, apologies for this chaos. I had an old college friend staying with me for far too long. He's only just left, so I haven't had time to get things in order."

He rushed about righting a fallen chair and scooping up empty glasses and bottles and incriminating balls of yellowed Kleenex. Clothes were everywhere. The musky smells of sex from last night lingered. Rich lit a candle.

"I'm Sam, by the way." The young man tried to retain his composure as he admired the view, pointedly giving Rich time to right the apartment.

"I know, you told me." He needed to re-assert himself, and the quickest way to do that was to get naked. Sam watched the reflection of Rich undressing in the window, pulling his own erection to life. Rather than embrace him, Rich pulled a bottle of white wine out of the refrigerator and slowly poured two glasses. As he drank from one, he positioned the other in front of his burgeoning cock. Turning toward Sam he said, "Would you like a drink?" Sam cocked a sideways grin and nodded. Throwing his tie over his shoulder he lowered himself and, looking up into Rich's masterful eyes, took a sip of wine while massaging the cock before his face with his other hand.

Rich watched their reflection in the window, the back of Sam's head bobbing up and down, their silhouette punctured by the skyline until the two images appeared as one. Windows streaked up his thighs, rooftops perched on the young man's shoulders. Sam stopped to take another swig and gently nuzzled Rich with his cheeks, nibbling at the taut foreskin gathered beneath his flange. Rich stepped back a half-step and set his own glass down. "Get undressed."

As Sam fervently obeyed, he walked over to review the stained wreckage of his bed. The box of chocolates was perched atop a pillow in the center of the mattress like a crown. He thought of the contents as edible jewels, but shadowy concerns flooded his mind when he opened the box. The cavities of velvet where the devoured chocolates had once resided resembled the dark, empty eye sockets of a skull. And here he was, about to spend more treasure…on a stranger. His hand hesitated over the invaluable contents. Suddenly, he craved chocolate madly.

Eyes closed, he brushed the truffles and candies with his fingertips and shuddered as the naked young man gripped his chest from behind and started kissing his way down Rich's spine. He picked a piece enclosed in emerald foil and unwrapped it as Sam spread his cheeks and kissed and licked his crevice, hot and sweaty from their walk. He shook his butt a little, signaling his partner to disengage while he stepped up onto the bed, the black medallion of chocolate on his tongue. Sam bounded up on the mattress as well, steadying himself by gripping Rich's forearms. They kissed. Forcing the chocolate back and forth between their mouths unfurled complex layers of taste, at the center of which was a powerful mint.

Rich felt as if frozen sapphires were slicing into his tongue. He shivered as the cold consumed them. Sam, too, nearly buckled and had to be held up. They clung to one another for warmth as the temperature in the room dropped. Outside, the sun set rapidly and was replaced by black clouds. The wind audibly picked up as snow fell, obscuring the city lights. They marveled that their breath was visible and frosty. They continued kissing for warmth and, impossibly, maintained their erections, poking and prodding into each other's bellies. Rich gripped the boy's rigid, squat dick, one of those rare beasts that more than made up what it lacked in length with a considerable girth. It was a source of heat, of life.

He bent to feed from it, to stave off the all-encompassing cold. The boy clutched his head and shivered as Rich took him into his mouth. And they slowly levitated above the bed. Rich held the boy to him as they gently floated. Loose lemons from the kitchen tumbled by. A fork slowly sailed through the air like an errant missile. The lamp drifted away from the wall, suspended in midair by its electrical cord anchor. Rich used the fulcrum of the cock in his mouth to spin his own body, stopping only when he was able to reach up and grab Sam's ankles, positioning his own demanding cock before the boy's face. He could feel a cold cheek warming against his elongated member as Sam clutched his calves and attempted to work Rich into his mouth.

They spun in unison, two hands on the same clock spinning slowly, forever in synch. The boy's fingers warmed Rich's legs as he felt his orgasm mount. He tightened his grip on Sam's calves to signal that he was ready and was surprised as the luscious, warm sperm coated the roof of his mouth, goading him to shoot his own load down Sam's willing throat. The momentum of their twin orgasms separated them and propelled them in opposing directions. Rich bumped the far wall and knocked his signed and numbered Nagel print askew (bought when he first moved to New York; he truly loved the artist during high school, having secretly worshipped Duran Duran while pretending to like NWA, though he now faked an ironic attitude whenever guests made a face at it).

The boy hit the headboard and slid to the mattress. The lemons dropped. The lamp took a nosedive and shattered its bulb on impact. Outside, the snowstorm evaporated as the late afternoon sun returned. Sam blinked repeatedly as Rich licked his cold and chapped lips. Each of them shivered. As the room temperature returned to normal, both could see their labored breath. He was about to offer the boy the warm renewal of a shower, but he thought better of it. He remained still to observe how Sam would react to what just happened.

After a few incoherent moments, he came alive and jumped about the room, stammering that that was the best sex of his life, that there must have been something in the chocolate, a hallucinogen, and he reached for the box of candy. Rich snatched it from his grasp, engulfed by a furious anger. His post-sex half smile twisted into a grimace. This was all that remained of his and Alex's relationship, and it was obviously magical. No mere *boy* was to handle it and likely defile these choice sacraments. He stared at Sam, who backed away toward his clothes piled by the window.

A number of perplexed emotions crossed the boy's face, Rich's malevolent silence daring each one to manifest itself with a question. It was too much. Sam quickly stepped into his clothes, shaking his head in bewilderment. Rich continued to glare until the boy shut the door behind him, his crumpled tie on the floor. Still unsatisfied, he listened with his ear against the door until he heard the elevator bell. Content only when the doors closed, muffling what he thought might have been a sneeze from Sam. Rich cradled the box of chocolates lovingly, hoping that the boy caught what would turn out to be a vicious cold.

Rich finished the bottle of wine but was hesitant to get dressed and go down for another. He didn't want to leave the box of chocolates alone. This was the essence of what he and Alex had had together; the sparks, the moments, had all been distilled and injected into these marvelous candies. Carefully, he had removed them one by one, felt the contours of each precious piece and sniffed at its concealed elements, trying to divine what sexual portals each might open. He was careful not to handle them for too long. He didn't want the sweat from the palms of his hands to melt any of the chocolate. Even though he was ravenous, he did not want to eat another, no matter the allure. Three pieces had been consumed so far. *When I finish the box, will I be able to forget about Alex? Did he have some Botanica witch cast a spell on a measly box of Duane Reade chocolates just to fuck with my head?* No, he knew that whatever was happening was more than poisoned candy. A lemon peeked out from under the bed. This was something special. *If I can't keep Alex, then I can at least keep this.* He rose, walked over to the refrigerator, emptied its scant contents into the shiny metallic trash can, pulled out all but the center shelf, and placed the box of chocolates within, as if it were a vault protecting his most cherished valuables. Resignedly, he dressed and went out. During the elevator trip down, he made a mental list of everything he needed to buy so he wouldn't have to leave the apartment again.

❖

Eventually, work stopped calling. Someone had fervently knocked at his door one afternoon, but he refused to even go to the peephole. Later, he admonished the doorman that absolutely no one was allowed up without his permission. When work didn't bother him anymore, he was able to turn his cell phone back on. Absentmindedly scanning the numbers in his phone, he was mildly depressed he couldn't find anyone he could share this magnificent discovery with.

All of his gay friends were former lays he'd kept in touch with hoping they would all secretly consider him "the one that got away." He thrilled at the idea that a small army desperate to please him was quartered in Chelsea, with a few minor outposts in Gramercy. They delighted at his every victory and hoped to one day yet again give him mastery over their modest domains. Not one of them would do in a situation like this. Each, in his own way, had despised Alex and would go to great lengths to evaluate this situation in an unfavorable light.

Nor would the few fag hags he retained be any better. Though all of them suffered from one eating disorder or another, none had an aversion to chocolate—just the opposite, in fact, judging from the likely results were he ever able to get one of them to actually mount a scale. Alex still hadn't called. He had thought about texting him a *Thnx 4 the chocolate*, hoping in vain to reconnect, savoring this powerful secret together, but he deeply feared the lack of any response. Not that he was alone.

A bevy of delivery boys were in and out of his apartment every day, as the refrigerator was now reserved for more important cargo than mere food. His lone excursion outside the apartment had been to load up on cash and liquor. Everything else had to be delivered. Even men. He craved sex and chocolate. Chocolate was his heroin. Men were his needle. And like every junkie, he cut his stuff out of necessity. He constantly ate horrible name-brand candy bars to stave off that strong desire to reach into the chilly, rarefied atmosphere of the refrigerator and sample from the heart-shaped box of chocolates. None satisfied, but at least they curbed his appetite for the more miraculous morsels forever beckoning.

The one rent boy he'd ordered online was serviceable, though the sex was off as he had justifiably eaten a portion of a truffle alone, just before his door rang. The darkest chocolate enthralled him as he let the hooker in and told him to undress. A velvety nighttime descended, all was shadowy and mysterious. What light shone from the candles flickered ominously. But as the older-than-he-looked-online boy shed his shirt and flexed his muscles beneath a moronic maze of tribal tattoos, he kept popping his gum. Naked, Rich had envisioned himself a vampire, the curtains behind him his cape, but since he didn't share the chocolate with the rent boy, it was hard to picture him as an anxious virgin. He seriously doubted any drug could render *that* effect. The guy clearly thought Rich was high on something and none-too-obviously looked around to see what he could steal. The night ended just okay, though Rich had to pay more, having bitten the boy on his back until he bled.

Since then, he approached the box of chocolates with intense trepidation. *Each time I eat one, I'm that much closer to finishing the box, and then where will I be?* He tried just licking one to no avail. They had to be partially or wholly consumed to work, and then they *worked*. A piece of chocolate wrapped around an unidentifiable nut took him to the Amazon River, where he masturbated in the shallows surrounded by menacing piranha. As all of his meals were delivered, he quickly realized one particular Chinese delivery boy lingered longer, touched his hand when the tip was given. After a few such encounters, he again ordered food from that restaurant. When the delivery boy entered, Rich stood naked in front of him, exact change in one hand, a piece of chocolate in the other. The boy blushed deeply, pocketed the money, and knelt to eat from Rich's hand. Rich was so turned on that he nearly forgot to keep some of the chocolate for himself, but as the boy turned his attention to Rich's stiffening member, he was able to salvage a large smear of creamy righteousness from his palm. They made bittersweet love under a light rain beneath edible marshmallow clouds. Bittersweet because the boy's antiquated beeper kept going off. He had more deliveries to make. They both came too quickly and parted longingly. The boy seemed not the least taken aback that his clothes were soaked. Rich tore up that restaurant's menu so as not to be tempted to share again.

And so it came that one relentlessly sunny afternoon, he found himself with only a single piece of chocolate left. It was improbably large and dark, a remarkable puzzle promising so much, but to solve it meant an end to everything. Naked, he studied the skyline at his window. The array of buildings was never quite knowable; every time he thought he'd mapped it all out, another skyscraper would be erected, or he would notice a rickety water tower he'd not previously incorporated into his memory. At night a familiar building's lights would come on in such a way as to transform it into a new and majestic structure.

He smiled his *I'm the catch of the day* smile at the city and turned toward the kitchen. Gently, he placed the box of chocolates on the counter. He wasn't surprised that it was just as heavy as when he first discovered it even though it now contained one piece. Pulling the lone shelf out from the refrigerator, he measured the white oblong box with his eyes. He clutched the red container, now soiled with so many of his dark, sticky fingerprints, under his arm. Rich gingerly put one foot in the refrigerator, pivoted on his heel and, as if taking a final bow, drew his other leg into the cold, benignly humming machine. Folding his body tightly, he closed the door behind him.

Overtime at the Beheading Factory

For his obligatory fifteen-minute break, Eddie stepped outside to be alone. The night was starless, the clouds low and exhausted. The square of dirt flanked by the factory and the warehouse was enclosed by a chain-link fence that rippled between the buildings. The distant parking lot seemed like an emerald mirage, a promise of escape toward endless adventures, the burnished gleam of every Escalade and pickup beneath the lights a magic lamp; but when they finally reached it after an eight-hour shift, claimants could only muster the desire for home, maybe pulling into Dunkin' Donuts on the way. Eddie lit a cigarette, exhaled, licked his dry lips and felt for change in his pocket. Once he'd been elected staff representative, he'd lobbied hard for soda and snack machines to supplement the grim coffee in the break room, yet he never seemed to have any change. Another drag. Unperceivable shifts of gray among the clouds above. The break whistle shook the metal door. He drilled the cigarette butt into moist, black dirt and went back inside.

❖

Like nearly everyone else on the night shift, he had started at the factory on the day shift: young, smug, thinking this was a temporary gig on the way toward a career that never materialized, keen on the reliable paycheck, yearning for nothing more than the next weekend and a new car. Car payments, marriage, and children eventually made the time-and-a-half the night shift paid look like a gold ladder out of a deep well of debt. He donned his protective face mask and pulled on his rubber gloves, nodding to his colleagues shambling out of the break room. Not one of them had said anything about the soda or snack machines. It wasn't his fault insurance copays went up again this year, but everyone sure made time to grumble to him about that.

Eddie took his spot and saw the team was in position, so he pressed the power button. The disassembly line shook to life. Units slid down the conveyer belt facedown, naked, trussed and gagged, rolled into place. He pulled the lever down and severed the head from the body. His partner Lucy, an older woman with manly shoulders and stout legs, swiftly hooked the twitching body into the chute as the surprised cranium flipped into the waiting cart. A steady flow of units, and when the cart was full, Louis ambled up with a replacement bin and wheeled the full one through the slit of the giant rubber curtain that led to the warehouse. Eddie was again annoyed by the looks on the faces in the cart: the fluttering eyelids, the silent, guppy-like opening and closing of mouths. *It's not like your copay just went up*, he thought.

Louis always took his time, headphones squeezing his dull skull like he didn't have a care in the world, often showing up just as the cart was about to overflow. Eddie and Lucy would look at each other and shrug. Last year, Eddie was Lucy's Secret Santa. Not knowing what to get her, he'd asked his wife. She picked up a pair of earrings at Sears, and Lucy had worn them every shift since. They were as tight as a team could be, and yet she never so much as mentioned the new vending machines, though a break didn't go by when she didn't have a Twix and a Diet Coke.

Frankly, he had expected his turn as staff representative to be more fulfilling. Eddie had walked into that first meeting with a list of reasons why their shift deserved overtime during the holiday crunch and spring season. Instead, he was presented with some startling numbers in terms of overhead. Management relied on him more than he'd expected, shared more business information with him than he'd cared to receive, and after six months, all he'd been able to net his team were the snack machines while just barely preserving their precious dental insurance.

With the thirty-minute whistle, Eddie switched hands, gripping the handle with wild relief as one set of tendons and muscle was torched by adrenaline while the other arm collapsed, a rusted crane, junkyard-doomed, yet mechanically resurrected with the next thirty-minute whistle. Eight more whistles, and he would head home, often meeting his wife on the lawn as she headed to work. They would chat about the children. She'd remind him breakfast was waiting for him on the table, to move the clothes from the washer to the dryer. She wouldn't kiss him if he had blood and gristle in his beard, so he'd wash up right there on the grass with the garden hose, spraying tracheal muck from the bottom of his boots. That wet kiss, the smell of her hair, the pancakes waiting with golden lozenges of butter oozing down the sides, the bad drawings taped to the refrigerator, all kept him going.

❖

Eddie turned out of the parking lot tired but content. He felt a certain peace driving home with the window down as the sun rose, natal dew clinging tenderly to the side view mirror, only to bead and erupt into oblivion as he picked up speed on the highway. For all his problems at work, his team consistently moved more units than the day shift. The night shift attracted an older, more serious crew—people like him with second mortgages and college funds to worry about. And at night, the units were more subdued and moved down the line quicker. Sometimes they flowed like salmon. His colleagues had no idea how good they had it. In his father's day, you didn't pull a salary, much less insurance. Back then you were paid by the head.

He remembered his father's hands. So much blood got under his nails that they permanently browned. This was decades before OSHA required gloves. His father had always looked wan around Christmas, cheeks sallow and drawn, having put in monumental amounts of overtime to earn enough to buy Eddie and his brothers the red wagons they so desperately desired, the sharp and shiny Erector Sets they demolished the cardboard packaging to get at. The miniature guillotines dutifully assembled on the shag carpet worked after some subtle direction from Dad. They practiced on one another's fingers, trying to hold back the tears if the dull metal of the makeshift blade happened to knock a knuckle. Now his own sons clamored for the controls of the video game version, shouting from the breakfast table as he came into the house, eager to impress with their latest high scores, how they played online against kids in other countries, besting a boy in Osaka just the other day.

THE LOVE OF THE EMPEROR IS DIVINE

In vino sanitas
—Pliny the Elder

Loyal Publius,

The love of the Emperor is Divine.

So said one of my eunuch procurers to the last little tasty morsel shoved into my chambers. At least this one had been bathed. His tidy tunic was loose. No doubt he'd been thoroughly searched by the Praetorian Guards. Emperors fear assassins the way rabble fear indigestion. As you have dutifully reminded me before, I am nearly the oldest emperor to wear the Purple. Real danger is a slippery set of stairs. If the daggers come, so be it. As long as I don't have to appear before the Senate again and accept their marbled accolades, beneficial poems, and painted statues that portray me as stronger than I have ever been in my life, more resolute and of sounder character than I'd actually care to be—a modern Seneca. Lo! If I live any longer, they'll carve statues of me riding chariots drawn by eagles while farting out golden apples of wisdom. Ridiculous. I want strong wine. I want Her Most Rotund Royal Highness to keep to her wing of the palace and the occasional kiss from a sweet boy. The right kiss, and I think of Decimus and our carefree school days in Greece. Do you remember him? I've no idea of his fate.

I am told by mutual acquaintances you appear withdrawn and depressed since your banishment to Naples. Well done. The more solitary and disgruntled you appear, the more likely you will draw sour serpents from their nests. How the discontent love to compare wounds, squeezing out verbal pus to smear on one another's lips and compare the pungent taste. Pay attention to the wives of the summering senators, especially old ones with patrician blood. Boredom loosens tongues, and they know their wealthy father's business as well as their husband's, so there's double bounty to be had.

I know your accommodations are among the most superior along the coast, as my uncle's freedman once owned the very villa you're in. Who knew that rascal would flourish so financially once the yoke was lifted? His daughters are still whores, however. You can only polish rotten fruit so much. I expect you to start complaining in earnest by autumn. No doubt a suitable crisis, real or imagined, will present itself, and you will be recalled. Until then, please pout and do not share the case of Narbonne wine that accompanies this missive. Importantly, when you decant, save and reuse the corks. I went to a lot of trouble to have them treated to maintain aroma and keep the wine from turning.

Report only salacious gossip and rumors of plot. I have no need for compliments. I am old, and my reign will be brief. The Empire is between wars. Our borders have grown and shrunk, expanded and withdrawn, an empire out of breath, an exhausted puffer fish caught in the net of history. Tired of assassinations, rattled by plague, with new religions racing up our backside like a mad rash, the Senate has hoisted this diadem upon my withered brow precisely because I look as worn out as the world feels.

Burn this letter and do not copy your reply. Our discretion maddens my secretaries with fears of conspiracies, and I do like to keep these eunuchs guessing.

Your Most Appreciative Emperor

Loyal Publius,

How does the clipping of testicles pull one's nostrils skyward? I've rarely seen a mincing eunuch who didn't throw his nose up in the air at any task. The one who brings me my boys does so as if delivering dirty linen to the laundry. Think how past emperors would have had him crucified, or worse. But I've decided my short reign will be a peaceful one. My singular goal is to adopt the right heir, to find a bright young philosopher with a democratic soul to return Republican principles to Rome. I am powerless in the present, yet the whim of succession shapes the world! And lo the princes and knights that leave their wives in my presence, thinking to divorce their way to the throne! Uglier are the ones who bring their ephebes around, the blond wisp of a beard tickling their curious and noble chins.

The poets of this age, or at least in this city, are humorless. If you find a wit on your end of the world, send him my way, please. I'll stand him dinner every night of the year for the chance to utter an unexpected laugh. These evenings of stale theater and watered-down wine will be the end of me. A novel idea: assassination through boredom. Nero tried it on the world, so perhaps the world now exacts its revenge regardless who occupies the throne.

Your last letter was interesting. You speak of recent dreams of Decimus? That you have nighttime visitations from one so fair speaks that the sap still runs through your veins. I envy you. It now takes greater effort on my part to summon what used to flow so freely.

Later this month, a party of senators from Hispania Ulterior will decamp from Rome and borrow Bassianus's estate. Get invited to one of their evenings of frivolity. I hear they're quite bawdy, and I would like a firsthand report. Your last letter was interesting but hard to read. I've enclosed my favorite ink and will have more sent. I find it thicker and less blotty than what the Imperial stores provide. Ignore the red tint when first brushed on papyrus; it dries to an ebony hue.

Again, burn this letter and do not copy your reply. I don't want future ages studying our drivel and gossip as if it were sagely advice the way scholars sort poor Claudius's material.

Your Most Jealous Emperor

Loyal Publius,

The feverish weather oppressing Rome makes your seaside villa more appealing than ever before. Half the city wants for banishment as luxurious as yours! Thank you for the complete works of Claudius. They've only just arrived and are as musty and droll as your wit. Next time you are at the market, look among the latest coins for my image on the new sestertius. My likeness is that of a crone. Even the laurels look withered. I blame this heat.

I approve of your lonely walks on the beach in the morning. This invites approach. No chance of being overheard. Wise move. Make sure your sandy march takes you past that churlish old equestrian Ligus's tiny villa. He's an early riser and blames me for the increase in last year's grain tax.

No, I do not remember Decimus as anything more than a harmless plaything. And playthings do not cry blood when they embrace you. Don't blame the Narbonne for your bad dreams, my friend. This comes with old age. Unspent lust piles up and pours back out under the crack of whatever nocturnal door it was secured behind. These carnal thoughts never die but ferment into an ugliness that requires the company of youth. Buy some young, choice slave. Treat him unjustly in the linen closet, and you'll sleep deeply and soundly, like the babe you just spoiled.

Your Most Exhausted Emperor

Loyal Publius,

I'm glad you have heartily renewed your approval of the wine. More is on the way. Your description of the Hispanus party was exact. Daresay our scribes at the courts could use a lesson from you! I have a small favor to ask. I've included a scroll I need discreetly returned to Proconsul Gnaeus's library. It's fragile and dusty, as he collects the works of obscure Stoic philosophers. Return the scroll to his household upon receipt of this missive, before the Hispanus party departs. Inquire if the Proconsul or any guests are summering there. Try to appear as if you're begging for a dinner invitation and explain that you borrowed the scroll summer before last. Gnaeus is currently touring Gallia to wean his son off a rather serious predilection for Roman harlots, and I would like to ascertain if he indeed lent his house out and, if so, to whom. Our spies have information that the Hispanus senators are in Neapolis for a clandestine meeting with unknown parties. Have no fear, you were at his house two summers ago, and he pleaded with you to borrow this particular text, so cover is provided—Gods, the eyes of these Imperial agents are everywhere! They even have record of that trip to the Isle of Rhodes we took while still so young. Also recorded, the name of the girl you abandoned me there for, as well as her height, hair color, and even a general appraisal of her teeth. I learned a lot puttering around the ruins of old Tiberius's playhouse, though I'm sure you learned more when you finally caught up with her in the port of Misenum. Yes, that's in the Imperial records as well, and so too are some of the gymnastics the two of you tried out in bed. It's both thrilling and startling to think we had caught the eye of Empire at that age. No word on Decimus in any of these scrolls, however, as if the spies and secretaries knew he'd come to naught.

Concerning your stated worry over the recent arrests and reassignments among the Praetorian Guard: don't try to make sense of it because it doesn't make any sense. I find it valuable to throw a little chaos at our military minds. They cannot comprehend anything that doesn't fit their chessboard vision of order and armor, so they read endless meaning into the occasional, random execution. If they're looking over their shoulder, then they're not looking for the throne.

Your Most Nostalgic Emperor

Loyal Publius,

I've started composing my letters to you late at night. The air is still hot, but no supplicants, slaves, or aggrieved citizens roam the halls. Their bustle and complaint agitates the very temperature of Rome. Did you know that during summers past, the Emperor Domitian had ice hauled down from the Alps? Nerva put a stop to that, and I concur. Nothing incites a rabble so much as obscene luxury in the face of their suffering. I find myself obsessed with past rulers and sympathetic toward those I had once considered vile. I was drafted into this lonely collegium and am now on the inside looking out, a prisoner of lisping litigants and petitioners weeping over the border skirmishes of countries I did not previously know were clients of the Empire.

Palace life is not like I imagined. I do not rule the world, I merely keep its accounts. I go to bed late and wake up early, and in between, I dream I am adding my seal to heaps and heaps of documents. Unlike you and your unseemly tussles with Decimus, I never dreams of boys or, even more obscenely, the Gods like I used to in the days of old. I used to dream in the Roman tongue, then Greek, and now I dream in figures, revenues, taxes, duties. Speaking of duties, it is not news that you report Quintus despises me. Find me the envious, those are the snakes which bite. I don't care about those that only hiss and shake.

I miss the sea air and long to join you. Make an offer to the Gods for me, I beseech you. Use the incense I have enclosed. Do not be put off by its powerful fragrance. The scent is designed for otherworldly nostrils.

Your Most Nocturnal Emperor

❖

Loyal Publius,

Thank you for your lifetime of friendship and service to the Empire. Your ready advice and willing ear have served my rise and have much benefited the throne. I'm sure by now news of the conspiracy and summary executions has reached you, and I know that everyone, even the favored, fear for their throats at moments like these. I've experienced my own night sweats as the Purple passed from one bearer to another in our eternally uncertain city. Be calm. Keep reading. No daggers are intended for you.

I never told you how I killed my father. It's an interesting story, not fraught with moral drama, nothing remotely Sophoclean about it, really, just pure calculation. I knew early on I was born to the Purple. Late one night as a small child, I woke from my crib without a cry or a start, and looked out the window to see lightning, but I heard no thunder. It was a marvelous vein of gold. Though it lingered in the sky for only a moment, it was forever burned itself into my mind. I knew it was the whip of Jove goading me on toward my fate.

From youth, I understood that my family's station exacerbated the situation, that if I reached for the throne, it would be denied. I would have to wait until it was offered. Father was my sole obstacle. I know you are shocked to read this, find it unfathomable. Please, have that last glass of Narbonne and know the tears I shed when we both learned of his death were real. It pained me greatly to remove my progenitor from my path, but the goal was mighty, and his good health and relative youth as well as his thrifty management of our estates were my greatest impediments. When he died, I inherited all. I quickly sold our vineyards in Gallia at a good price to our neighbors, the formidable but financially struggling Amlianus family, and their gratitude propelled me into the arms of their oldest, humorless daughter.

Our marriage was my introduction to the social strata where I met my second wife, but you are already familiar with these stories. What you never knew was how purposeful our youthful wanderings were to me. When you dabbled in Cypriot whorehouses, I visited the last living tutor of Marcus Aurelius. You should have stayed longer on Rhodes, Publius, for there my real education began. At a dingy bookstall, I stumbled upon the diary of Tiberius's eunuch procurer. I devoured the secrets within. Aside from the devious acts he committed on behalf of the mad Emperor and the frightful errands he ran for other members of the twisted Julian line, he rather offhandedly recorded how he gathered the components of an ancient Sumerian spell the Emperor's mother, the inimitable Livia Drusilla, utilized to exert control from behind the throne.

Your role in uncovering the conspiracy against the royal personage was invaluable. The scroll you returned to Gnaeus's estate was quickly found to belong to Bassianus, as I knew his astute personal librarian would examine the document and see the intended inscription. He attempted to deliver it himself and was arrested by the Praetorian Guards at Bassianus's gates. The scroll was again reviewed there in full public view of the astonished Hispanus party and shown to contain a secret map of the royal bedroom as well as the schedule of my guards. Word travels fast. Bassianus opened his wrists before the guards could remove him from his modest mansion on the Aventine Hill. The trial for the Hispanus conspirators will be a quick one. The confiscation of their estates will go a long way toward satiating the ravenous Imperial budget. Narbonne is not cheap, my friend.

I have always hated Gnaeus.

But what of Father? On his birthday, I sent him the same rare ink you have been using yourself. On Lupercalia, I sent him wine of moderate expense, infused with the same herbs I had sprinkled into yours. I had the household slaves burn the required incense in his presence. The dust you inhaled from the Bassianus scroll was of the same substance mixed into the powder my mother brushed her cheeks with, the cheeks he dutifully kissed every morning before inspecting the farm. These ingredients, when delivered in the right order, serve as an aphrodisiac for my alphabetic demon. Oh, I've sent him everywhere! Britannia. Cyrenaica. A fitting way to dismiss those whose service is no longer required. The elements needed to amass Pluto's ink practically require the resources of an empire to draw upon, yet another reason to assume the Purple. My minion travels flat on the page, painted black letters that only rise when summoned. Summoned by your poisoned breath, Publius. I've only seen this dark rising once, when I perfected the process on unsuspecting Decimus. He's the only soul to ever read one of my poor attempts at poetry. He must have thought it my attempt to win his favor—when he clearly favored you. To mock me, the creature now takes his form, or the shadow of a nightmare thereof. Or so I am told. I do not dream of Decimus. He refuses me still. And so I sent him to you.

Watch the ink, slippery as an eel, thin as a knife blade, black as a sibyl's cunnus, leap from the papyrus and take form. It pulled Decimus's lips apart and forced its way down his throat. The thing will worm its way through your innards, until it reaches your mind, your heart—to leave you stricken as if by apoplexy.

I can imagine the discomfort you are feeling now. It's not the effect of nerves or wine that makes the page shimmer so. The ink is reaching for you now. This is one letter you needn't burn. As the words rise from the page, the parchment turns to ash.

Your sacrifice immeasurably improves the Empire. When word reaches Rome of your demise, I won't be alone in being distraught. The panegyrics I will commission on your behalf will be a rallying point for the citizenry to put this horrid assassination plot behind us. I'll erect a statue of your likeness in the very Senate we both so despise. You will stand there forever, a pale immortal. Seashells will adorn the base, symbolizing your philosophical, ruminative nature, your oceanic wisdom. Upon viewing this marble masterpiece, the masses will all exclaim a singular sentiment—

The love of the Emperor is Divine.

Rising Sons

A s the monk reached for the boy's shirt collar, the sound from the giant bell shook the wispy bamboo surrounding the shrine and reverberated throughout the iron mountains. He was the youngest monk there, and he snuck in a game of soccer with the students at the nearby high school whenever he could. Confident, agile, he was fast and should have been able to bring his round-faced quarry to the ground, but he hesitated and the child slipped through his fingers. The boy gleefully put all of his weight into the post that hung before the bell. Sunlight played across its ancient bronze surface like bits of diffused dandelion, like whispered prayer. The young monk had questioned his faith of late, had smoked a cigarette after the last furtive soccer match, and at night thought more about girls with white lipstick and McDonald's hamburgers than sutras.

The post struck the bell and it sounded *wrong*. It groaned. It exhaled decades of breath rank with unmourned loss. Emerald bamboo shivered. The young monk closed his eyes and reflexively bowed an apology to the seated statue of Buddha as the senior monk struck the boy forcefully with a broom. The boy's astonished father turned from yelling at him to shouting at the elder monk. The mother shouted both her husband's and the child's names, but the young monk heard neither as the earth lurched. He in turn shouted "Earthquake!" almost with an exclamation of relief, that whatever had come out of the bell now had a name and could be dealt with.

Monks poured out of their quarters and most fell to the ground in prostration. Younger monks stood in doorways and braced themselves. The more devout, who took to heart the constant admonishment that the bell should *never* be struck a fourth time or the angry army of suicides buried beneath the shrine would wake, knelt and prayed.

Hidden from history, the largest mass seppuku ever carried out was purposefully forgotten, for it had tragically happened after the war ended. Lines of communication were frayed. The aged general had not yet been informed of the treaty, and upon sighting of American troops, he ordered his starving soldiers to commit suicide, many of them in their early teens, young Hokkaido farmers who'd never seen Tokyo. They were buried hastily, the Emperor charging a neighboring cloister of monks with appeasing their restless spirits. He gave them an ancient bell from the Kamakura period, one designed to appeal to the ravenous spirits of disgraced samurai. Locals came to pray and burn incense on certain holidays, but tourists like these were rare.

And it *was* an earthquake—one of dark fists breaking through the slightly rounded mounds of moss encircling the modest temple. The corpses of soldiers pulled themselves from their mass grave and wavered on unsteady, spindly legs roped with the rotting cloth of bloodstained uniforms. Wave after wave of blackened skulls ascended. Each soldier had two mouths. Clotted dirt dripped from between teeth and poured out of the foolish grin of sword-split stomachs. Hungry mouths, having bled out for Emperor and country, were ravenous from a diet of earth and incense. The mother dropped to her knees and frantically rummaged through her silver Fendi bag, as that's where all the answers usually were. The father took pictures with his phone as the horde fell upon the monks and feasted on their shaved heads like so much soft mochi ice cream. The young monk grabbed the broom that the older monk had dropped and hoisted it above his head as if it were a sword and looked to put himself between the child and the dead soldiers already mounting the stairs. Yet the boy had already retrieved his new Nikes from the temple antechamber and fled down the stony path, threading faded torii desperate for a new coat of red paint.

HONEYSUCKLE

Honeysuckle was buck-toothed and knobby-kneed, with needle-thin arms and weedy broken wings. The size of an infant, with his protruding teeth and weak chin, he looked more rodent than faery. Once-glittering gold flesh now hung like a jaundiced kite caught in a sickly tangle of bent and brittle branches. His eyes were bulbous yet somehow recessive, dark slits of intense suspicion that would widen into goldfish orbs of fear whenever he felt trapped, threatened, or was in withdrawal from crystal meth. He spent his days scrounging for cans and bottles to sell at the recycling plant across town. Nights were spent smoking meth in the backseat of a rusted car abandoned at the bottom of a hill in the sparse woods behind a giant Publix grocery store in Tallahassee.

The elfin Honeysuckle didn't make enough money from the cans and bottles to pay for his drugs. To make up the difference, he ran errands for other, slightly more affluent addicts, mostly humans whose welfare checks and entrepreneurial efforts, like holding methadone in their mouths and selling it to other addicts outside the clinic on Magnolia Street, gave them access to more cash. He would fetch them cigarettes from the one farm store that would sell to faeries. He had let them use his teeth as a bottle opener, but on the side he also sold his snot. Faery snot has certain hallucinogenic properties that didn't appeal to the hard drug users who camped out behind the Publix, but it did attract a certain, minute number of college students, kids interested in Wicca and all things faery. They'd pay through the nose for fey snot.

He rarely had repeat customers, though. Drugs and hard living had diluted the potency of his snot. Usually his college student consumers saw a few blinking lights, heard a smattering of distant flute music, and that was it. Still, he was often their first contact with faery folk, so their enthusiasm sometimes colored their experience. Faery snot had to be consumed, and his was so viscous and sticky that he advised his customers to spread it over a cracker. One of his few regulars, a large girl with tiny pink pimples on her cheeks and a natty macramé shawl wrapped around her shoulders, always smeared the snot on an Oreo. That first time, her eyes rolled back in her head as she exhaled in ecstasy. Now Honeysuckle craved sweets almost as much as meth, and he thought about snatching the rest of the cookies from her, but he was too worried she was going to pass out in the backseat of the abandoned car or fall over and crush him. Ever since then, he tried to peddle his snot by the Dumpsters behind the Publix.

Winters in Tallahassee were cold and damp, the opposite of what he had imagined Florida to be. Honeysuckle tried to shield himself from the wind by ducking between stacks of flattened cardboard boxes. Bits of rotten vegetable matter blackened the ground surrounding the Dumpster. The sun had set, and he held out desperately for one last customer before he retired to the promise of singed bliss in a glass pipe. The night's chill deepened as a fox sauntered past on his hind legs, pulling a petite set of luggage on wheels behind him. The fox sniffed disapprovingly and curled its orange-blond tail in disgust before plunging into the thinning underbrush. Honeysuckle paid him no mind, knowing the urbane faery folk of Atlanta were in retreat. Most passed through Tallahassee on their way to safer and warmer climes. As if on cue, a wind-battered flyer landed at his feet: a missing faery poster. *Have You Seen Me?* The photocopied picture showed a curious infant elf, wide-eyed, enchanting. The smudged bottom of the sheet listed height, weight, identifying marks, and an incantation to summon anxious parents. Honeysuckle mouthed the incantation silently to himself, knowing that the parents had never been called, the child never found. Something was taking faeries in Georgia, and it had been going on for a while, necessitating an unheard of exodus from the Big Peach. The wind picked up again and pulled the flyer back into the darkness. Honeysuckle sniffed, was about to wipe his nose and thought better of it. Best to reserve his stock in case a hippie-straggler showed up. He stoically snorted and guffawed, holding on to his only oozing resource as the bitter fingers of winter silently strummed the harp of his useless wings.

❖

Lighter to pipe then gray smoke. Coarse heat filed away at his cracked and peeling lips, and Honeysuckle forgot everything. Then he remembered. Honeysuckle remembered the perfect valley. Feathery green grass and sunlight filtered through flowers the color of amber, if amber only encapsulated happiness and frolic. Dandelions exploded in the air and froze, a ballet of wishes and whispers and faery song. Honeysuckle exhaled and gulped as he opened his eyes to twisted windshield wipers framed by broken glass. Shreds of plastic bags convulsed in the leafless limbs of the trees—a mute chorus of battered ghosts. Honeysuckle hit the pipe again, and a tear rolled down his cheek as entry back into the valley was denied, no matter how tightly he closed his eyes and pulled the meth down into his lungs or up into the parched folds of his brain.

❖

Traffic ebbed in and out of the parking lot that hugged the bland strip mall. Honeysuckle hugged himself and wished he had a pair of sunglasses to block out the glaring sun and the annoying, open-mouthed stares of children pulled along by aggravated mothers as he leaned against the cement-encased trash can outside of the TCBY. A junkie had promised to buy him a white chocolate mousse waffle cone with sprinkles if he provided some manual release—Honeysuckle was forever thankful that his giant teeth kept his addict brethren from seeking additional services. However, enough time had passed that he worried his benefactor had overdosed in the bathroom. Distant sirens confirmed this suspicion, so he sulked away toward the bus stop, hoping to bum enough quarters along the way for a ride back to the encampment.

Honeysuckle's abode in the backseat of a car was near a ragtag tent city of the homeless, addicts, and the occasional down-on-its-luck faery. Though he preferred solitude, the closeness of his fellow vagabonds provided Honeysuckle with a measure of safety, plus the economy of trade and favors tapped him into a steady supply of meth. Unable to score enough quarters for the bus, he walked the whole way home, enduring insults and the occasional beer bottle thrown from cars. By the time he got back, darkness had fallen, and the homeless men and women of the encampment huddled around a low fire shielded from the road by thin trees, a hodgepodge of shopping carts, and grimy tarps.

Honeysuckle sought out Decayla, the only other faery folk currently in residence. She had made the mistake of falling in love with a human whose alcoholism and schizophrenia had cost him his job and their home. Now they lived in a tent jammed with paperback books, trash bags filled with clothes, and their mangy terriers, Agnew and Mondale. Her husband snored, his latest wire notebook manifesto thick with manic scribblings open across his chest. Sleeping dogs warmed his feet. Tiny Decayla hovered above him. The beat of her black butterfly wings did little to diffuse the smell of dirty laundry, body odor, and pot smoke. Decayla was a Wispie, a rare species of faery that dined on fanciful verse and nonsense rhyme, making the fractured thoughts of her spouse a veritable salad of addictive insanity. She feasted on his words and was made drunk whenever he veered toward the conspiratorial, which was often. Honeysuckle parted the tent flap and motioned for her to come outside, but she shook her thick and tangled dark mane and waved him in. He sighed and stepped into the claustrophobic mess. The dogs stirred as Decayla absentmindedly turned her attention back to the madness written in the notebook below.

"If it's a bad time, I can come back later," he grumbled, but didn't make a move to leave.

She clutched the edged of the stained doily she wore as a dress and curtsied, then lowered herself to sit on top of the nearest dog's head. She blinked as if waking from a restful nap. Dark mascara encircled her eyes, accentuated porcelain skin interrupted by slivers of blue vein.

"So sorry, love, but whenever he writes about the gold standard, my wings curl."

"Yeah, well I got screwed over by a trick at the TCBY and had to walk home. I was hoping you'd front me something sweet." He tried to blink his eyes back at her, feigning coy innocence. He looked as if he were having a stroke instead.

Alarmed, Decayla took flight and disappeared within the

folds of a crumpled army jacket. She reappeared, laboring beneath the weight of a caramel square, finally dropping it with relief into his cupped hands. Honeysuckle ripped the wrapper off as Decayla stole a glance at her spouse's fanatical drivel. Satiated, he shared a menthol cigarette with the other faery and made small talk by candlelight until Decayla could no longer bear to be away from the tempting manifesto, so Honeysuckle said his good-byes and departed. He decided to try and sell some snot before crawling into the abandoned car for some much-needed sleep. He had been awake for days, high on meth, and the candy he had just devoured helped bring him down. A light drizzle poked at the plastic sheeting much of the camp used for roofs and patted the few remaining leaves in the trees overheard, nearly dissuading Honeysuckle from his trip to the Dumpster. He only had a few quarters, though, and knew if he was fortunate enough to sleep through the night, he would wake with a powerful craving for the drug, so it was better to start tomorrow financially ahead.

By the time he reached the Dumpster, the rain had stopped. A single floodlight cast an emerald hue on a stack of packing crates. He slouched into his usual position and hoped if any customers came to buy snot, they'd do so soon, and that they didn't know the going price so he could charge them double. Moths played within the beam of light as Honeysuckle dozed. He slid to the ground and woke with a start as he bumped his head on the Dumpster. No cars or giggling college students approached. Still, something felt different. He thought maybe a stealthy raccoon had traipsed past, and he was about to head home when he noticed a single cookie had been placed on the ground, dead center in the pool of light. Honeysuckle's eyes narrowed as he scanned the darkness, but he was alone. He approached cautiously—it was an Oreo, his favorite. Without hesitation, he snatched it up and gobbled it down. He couldn't believe his luck! That and the caramel made this a day of victories. He sucked the crumbs from between his teeth and wondered if one of his regular customers, maybe that large girl, had left it for him when he noticed another cookie just outside the circumference of light.

Honeysuckle looked around. The moths were gone, the dust from their wings slowly filtered out from the safety of the light and into the darkness. Awake for days, lulled into a false sense of security from a sugar high, he grabbed at the Oreo and was about to eat it when he noticed yet another, placed beneath the bumper of a parked delivery van. Fearful a raccoon could easily emerge from the nearby woods to devour it, he leapt toward his target without thinking. He was so delirious with joy, having stuffed both cookies in his mouth, closing his eyes to better savor the soot of chocolate crumbs coating his drug-numbed tongue, he never heard the van doors swing open. As the sack dropped over his head and tightened around his neck, Honeysuckle choked and thought to claw his unseen kidnappers as he was pulled into the back of the van. The engine roared to life. The taste of exhaust overpowered the creamy taste of the cookies as he heard the doors shut. Laughter followed, then an incantation, and though he struggled, sleep crept over him like a wave of spiders.

Anger and fear and his own rank breath inflated the hood over his head. He'd tried resignation, he'd tried pleading, and he'd even tried to peddle his snot at considerable discount, but nothing had elicited so much as a peep from his captor. His internal compass told him they were headed north. The smoothness of the ride and the fact that they hadn't stopped or turned in hours meant they were on the freeway. As the spell wore off and fear and adrenaline erased his sugar high, withdrawal gnawed at his gut. If they were driving north, they were headed toward Georgia.

Whatever had been taking faeries in Atlanta had just taken a road trip, and he was the souvenir.

Honeysuckle rolled about on the floor of the van in frustration, half hoping his captor would strike him or say something. At least that way he might know if he was dealing with a human or a faery, and maybe learn how many they numbered. Silence greeted his protest. Wrapped in rage and dismay, with an overriding desire to lose himself in a fog of meth, Honeysuckle twisted and moaned. From the front of the van, he heard the turn signal engage as the vehicle slowed. Someone or something switched on the radio and the Mamas and Papas song, "Go Where You Wanna Go," filtered out, masking another incantation which lured the faery to sleep.

❖

Honeysuckle dreamt of the perfect valley, something he'd never been able to do before, necessitating his experiment with potions and spells and eventually drugs. He was willing to take anything, try any substance to return to those green gossamer veldts.

He dreamt his wings were full and working again, golden membranes that carried him over a field of blue rosebushes shading sleeping black lions. His cheeks were twin suns, his lips full and wet with laughter. He flew to the lake in the center of the valley to watch his love, Efran, work on their boat. He admired how the sweat and sawdust speckled his partner's muscular frame as he sanded down their ship and readied it for a trial run. The faeries had been brother-warriors during the troll wars, and peace had only deepened their bond. Since

Efran was a landed elf and had no wings, he put his superior carpentry skills into the boat's frame, while Honeysuckle, as an airy elf, was able to fly long distances and to great heights. He had coaxed the giant blind mountain worms to relinquish their rare silk. He lovingly sewed this silk into the fabric of the sail, imbuing their craft with the capability of flight. They had planned to sail to the stars together and drink the milk of the moon.

Honeysuckle always tried to sneak up on Efran while he was hard at work to steal a kiss or drop caterpillars into his jerkin, but the other faery sensed his approach and even from the greatest distance would stop working and turn to admire his lover in flight. In doing so, that fateful last day in the perfect valley, Efran failed to see a cluster of storm hornets materialize out over the lake. Storm hornets were an evil remnant of the troll wars, conjured to loosen the defenses of a fortress before attack.

Though the trolls were long vanquished, the smoldering insects lingered like land mines in the faery world, unpredictable and dangerous. Some were as big as bulls, others the size of the tiniest pebble—all could become intangible and were thus immune to sword and spear, making them nearly unconquerable. They streamed the blackest smoke, providing the perfect cover for assault. Honeysuckle shouted a warning that was carried away on the breeze as Efran waved and shook his head, thinking his lover was trying to play a trick on him. It didn't take long, however, for the faery to hear their wicked drone. Horrified by their burgeoning rush toward land, he dove under the craft just in time. Honeysuckle rushed into a thicket of trees, wishing desperately for a rain wand, the only known dispersant for storm hornets.

The roar of the creatures was deafening. He clung to a bending pine as smoke and the beat of insect wings nearly pulled him from safety. The stampede of startled deer and frightened fauns below added to the cacophony. Honeysuckle could not hear Efran's cries for help over the dark din, and he strained against the onslaught to aid his partner. Through the veil of storm hornets, he could see the angry insect cloud had managed to overturn the wooden boat, but Efran was nowhere to be seen. He thought he heard a shout from above. The magical sail they had sewn and stored in the bow of the boat had come free and risen above the tempest. Efran was hanging, upside down, hopelessly entangled in the rope and sail. Honeysuckle found a break in the storm and took his chance. If he could fly above the mass of hornets and catch up with Efran, together they could reel in the sail and land safely far from the tempest.

The sky grew clearer as he shot past the blackest stampede of hornets. Even better, Efran had seen him and was visibly relieved. He'd stopped struggling, knowing rescue was on the way. Loud buzzing pierced Honeysuckle's ears, and as he turned to gauge the distance of its source, a hovering storm hornet the size of a rat alighted on his chest and plunged its smoldering stinger straight through his heart. Pain beyond endurance spread through his body. The faery reached out to his lover, now pulled even farther skyward by wind and fate. Efran stretched out his hand in return as Honeysuckle convulsed and coughed out smoke. Twisting in agony, he threw off his attacker and succumbed as black fumes billowed out of his mouth. The sting of a storm hornet is not fatal, for it doesn't cut flesh, but instead rends time and space, opening up a random portal within the victim, who in turn vomits smoke until eviscerated and reconstituted elsewhere.

Honeysuckle woke up coughing under a pile of leaves in the Saint Augustine National Cemetery on Florida's east coast. It was the middle of the night. The surrounding palm trees, silhouetted by street lamps, swayed in resigned agreement with his dismal conclusion that he had been forcibly evicted from the perfect valley. The uniform graves of soldiers lined up to confirm that lost love is as universal as it is permanent.

❖

The caravan of mobile homes was insular and uninviting: human eyes perceived rusty buckets of squalor. Menacing Doberman pinschers tied to a chicken-wire fence guarded an array of weedy trash, an old washing machine, stacks of bald tires, and a nondescript van on cinder blocks. Humankind felt compelled to leave if they happened upon the site, and would have trouble remembering exactly where and when they stumbled upon the motley collection of trailers.

The fey perceived it differently: a patch of gigantic black pumpkins with small doors and windows carved into their exterior. A slanted stovepipe protruded from the largest, central pumpkin. The ebony gourds were protected by a tall and twisted wrought iron fence with sharp, filed points, and where human eyes saw mean dogs, coils of whip-fast kudzu writhed, ready to wrap and suffocate any interloper. Interspersed within the lush grass were faery bones. Honeysuckle viewed the whole scene from the window of the smallest pumpkin domicile where he hung suspended from a gold birdcage in the middle of the room.

Other cages of various sizes and suspended at various lengths from the ceiling hung empty. Honeysuckle gave not a thought to the fate of any previous occupants, nor was he concerned about the vicious kudzu outside. Every shelf and table within the hollowed-out pumpkin was stocked with jars and decanters of candy and sweets. No matter how often he surveyed their contents, he was forever discovering new treasure, sugar baubles to delight his palate. Pixie sticks promised previously unheard of potency. Taffies and truffles of rare hues and flavors nearly pulsed with saccharine possibilities.

He'd yet to meet his kidnapper but was grateful his cage had been filled with sweets. The floor below was a spent rainbow of wrappers and colorful crumbs. The sugar pulsing through his veins was a much deserved respite from the bartered candy bars and melting ice cream for which he had debased himself. To be imprisoned within a cornucopia of confection was just about an answered prayer. When the faery finally met his captor, the richness of his sweet imprisonment lost only a bit of its syrupy luster.

The rattle of keys barely distracted Honeysuckle from teething on a voluptuous lollipop which not only changed flavor but also tinkled out piano music with every lick. He looked up as the creature entered and unfolded its large frame, consuming most of the space within the pumpkin and knocking about several empty birdcages. Honeysuckle's eyes narrowed as his street smarts momentarily resurfaced. An enemy had made itself known. Trolls were infamous for their stupidity, but their armies didn't deploy and rearm themselves without some brainpower, which was what the subspecies of trollucants provided. Rarely encountered by other faery folk, trollucants were reclusive master planners as well as devotees of the black arts. The one that now filled the pumpkin was male, gangly with a cruel jaw. Thick spectacles obscured his gaze, and though green-skinned like all trolls, his hue was more ashen, as if he rarely left the pumpkin compound. *Or did so only at night*, Honeysuckle thought. He felt the sharpness of his mind struggle to the surface; the instinct toward observation and exploitation, which both kept him in and was diminished by meth, sizzled and popped.

The trollucant smiled and pulled a handful of butterscotch candies wrapped in gold foil from his pocket. The creature let them drop slowly into the cage. Honeysuckle forgot about his captivity as he caught each morsel, drooling as he clutched this new manna from heaven. He gorged as his kidnapper spoke with an abnormally thick diction, as if his tongue were too big for his mouth.

"Enjoy your treats, my little sweet, and know that you are my guest. Should you wish to leave your gilded cage, simply tell me the number of diamonds in the diamond jar."

Honeysuckle was too taken with the butterscotch to give the trollucant more than a cursory nod. He'd noticed the tall glittering jar earlier and assumed it was filled with swizzle sticks of rock candy. Teething on butterscotch, he narrowed his eyes as he studied the container. What he thought was mineralized sugar churned slowly, a heavenly martini of incalculable frozen worth, for the diamonds within changed as they spun. Certain facets birthed miniature jewels, while other large stones absorbed the smaller ones as easily as a large fish might gulp down sparkling minnows.

Honeysuckle blinked, nonplussed, and continued to dine on the smorgasbord melting in his hands. The trollucant nodded and licked his green lips with a thick and serrated black tongue. He took stock of the candy on the shelves, selected a few more choice morsels for his captive, dropped them in the faerie's cage, and departed. Honeysuckle's carriage swung as candy wrappers wafted toward the floor. The jangle of keys was the only reminder that he was a prisoner, and the future might not be so sweet.

An unknown number of weeks passed as Honeysuckle continued to revel in the joy of unending candied delights. The trollucant came by daily to deposit more sweets. He talked nonsense in a singsongy voice as he refilled jars and sprinkled goodies into the birdcage. Honeysuckle's appetite returned as he weaned off meth—he always finished the mounds of candy. He gained weight, a golden flush returning to his skin. His wings started to fill out again, and the trollucant joked that soon he'd be able to fly away, though they both suspected in another month or so, he would be too fat.

The trollucant would open the pumpkin's window, and the fresh air would steal the wondrous scents of so many sweets. Across the yard, Honeysuckle could see impatient movement within the largest of the ebony pumpkins. He was pretty sure the trollucant lived in the smaller pumpkin and his wife lived in the large one, but since she never left, he imagined she had gotten too obese to fit through the door. Sometimes he would hear them argue as the trollucant placated her with whispered promises. Chewing on taffy, he examined the bones in the yard, discarded as nonchalantly as the wrappers beneath his cage.

One afternoon it rained, and the trollucant was late in bringing Honeysuckle his candy. Bored and hungry, the faery did something he had never bothered to do before: he tasted his own snot. His steady diet of sugar had not only fattened him up, it had increased the thickness and strength of his snot. He thought it tasted like vermouth and was about to stick his finger back in his nose for another sampling when his eyes rolled toward the back of his head and he slumped over, gripped by a powerful hallucination.

❖

Above the perfect valley, white clouds haloed Efran's head like peaceful pillows. His lover's mouth was open, but Honeysuckle could not hear him above the din of the storm hornets. He wondered if his wings had regained enough strength. Maybe this time he would be able to rescue his love. The magic sail that had ensnared Efran unfurled farther and pulled him higher. Honeysuckle strained with all his might to rise as well and succeeded only in hearing what Efran said. This jolted him back to reality, but the dream continued as he closed in on Efran. Honeysuckle smiled at him with the deepest gratitude and a longing that would never go away but would never consume him again, either.

❖

Sparks intermingled with tears as the vision waned. The rain stopped. Honeysuckle swung the cage back and forth. When it was as close to the window as possible, the faery chucked one of the pieces of candy out into the yard. It landed among the bones, causing the violent kudzu to stir and coil tighter. A large, hungry shadow moved restlessly within the largest gourd. The remaining candy spilled out of the bottom of his cage as he continued to swing back and forth like an eager pendulum. When the trollucant finally emerged, he cooed as usual and mumbled pleasantries. This time he brought a small pail filled with a colorful assortment of jawbreakers. Honeysuckle feigned interest, and as the creature sprinkled candies into his cage, the faery clapped with counterfeit glee.

"Thank you so much for feeding me, Mr. Trollucant! I'd really like to repay your kindness some day."

The trollucant arched a black, caterpillary eyebrow, as Honeysuckle had never spoken before. He quickly adopted a benign expression. "Ho, ho, ho, that's very sweet of you. I'm, ah, sure me and the missus will think of, uh, something you can do for us soon."

He returned to restocking the candy jars as Honeysuckle continued.

"Well, I've imposed on you too long, so I guess I'll be going." He blinked innocently as the trollucant nodded in agreement.

"Sure, sure. Just tell me the number of diamonds in the jar, and you're as free as a phoenix!" It even managed to whistle a tune, as if they were talking of the smallest of matters.

"Oh, okay," Honeysuckle said slyly, "but only if you agree to switch places with me. I would really like to return the favor by showering you with treats as well!"

The trollucant laughed. "Of course! It's about time someone took care of me for a while. Just you let me know the number of diamonds in the jar."

The creature visibly relaxed, sure the imprisoned faery was powerless in the cage. But Honeysuckle knew the encampment of black pumpkins was a place of enchantment, and that fey pacts were binding. He closed his eyes and the image of Efran in the sky returned. He actually felt the wind on his face. He heard his words. How many times had they said that to each other? When they discovered love in the trenches, covered in mud and blood, he had first said them to Efran. At their binding ceremony, surrounded by faery friends encircled around the Endless Oak, they declared in unison, *You are the one for me.*

Honeysuckle gave the trollucant an intensely sober look and answered him.

"One."

The diamond jar swirled. The pearlescent dross of sugar disintegrated to reveal a single hard stone floating in the middle. The trollucant let loose a wet, mucus-filled roar as Honeysuckle was transported outside of the cage while his kidnapper appeared within, impossibly doubled over, arms dangling outside the bent bars. For all of the creature's weight, the chain from which the cage was suspended miraculously did not give. Honeysuckle spread his wings and took flight for the first time in a long time. As he buzzed about the room, knocking jar after jar of candy to the floor, the trollucant whined and rattled his cage in frustration, begging to be let out.

Honeysuckle flexed his buttery gold wings and bobbed in the air. "Wait, wait! You promised to feed me," the monster cried out. He greedily eyed the pieces of candy on the floor, interspersed with bits of broken glass from the toppled jars.

Honeysuckle flew out the door and up into the sky. Leapfrogging from cloud to cloud, he shouted earnestly over his shoulder, "Oh, I'll be back right after I find my sweetheart."

HALLOWEEN PARADE

The Halloween Parade in New York City is a sloppy pageant of mock mayhem and elastic shadows. Outer-borough boys in drugstore masks muffling beery breath push through the crowd to grope no small variety of ass in tight-fitting jeans. Tourists gape and take pictures as men in heels strut about in glamorous costumes so meticulous most Las Vegas showgirls would hang their sequined heads in shame. Everywhere Frankensteins, Draculas, and Wolfmen cavort with modern incarnations of fear: those cinematic flavors of the moment, disgraced politicians and goofy celebrities, interspersed within a sea of witches, some in elaborate dark robes and wielding scraggy brooms, others sporting nothing but a pointy hat, just enough to signify membership among the coven.

Stephen sifted the crowd as he performed his annual census. He relished this time of year, when adults snatched back the one holiday that mattered from greedy made-for-cavities children, this pagan night that celebrated frenzy and death and darkness. Stephen kept Halloween alive throughout the year by meticulously maintaining his collection of horror films and memorabilia. He purchased horror movies of all stripes, running through countless phases, grabbing up the reissues, the director's cuts, jumping on gory bandwagons galore. Asian cinema was big a few years ago, and he'd lost count of the number of spooky bootlegs he'd gathered in Chinatown featuring ghost girls streaming black hair. He had reverently replaced his vast VHS collection one by one as the format was superseded by DVD, cherishing those grainy slasher and monster films yet to be rereleased on disc. Halloween was a stake in the ground around which his whole year swung, and Stephen counted the killers at the parade every year.

Men his age grew up during the slow death throes of the drive-in and the materialization of malls, a time when new monsters emerged from the primordial soup of spilt-sodas-and-semen sludge of the Times Square grindhouse floors to flex their cold, pale biceps into the McDonald's-like arches of verifiable franchises. Stephen's bespeckled, buck-toothed youth was spent far from the football field, within suburban multiplexes, air-conditioned darkness wrapping him in a comfortable cloak of maintainable fear. Fear he could control, a twin to the longing he was desperate to explore yet also hide and restrain, longing linked to sin and a deserved death by the newspapers reporting a new "gay cancer."

Three man-shaped killers tore themselves from the screen in his youth, pushing past poorly masked stranglers, mutants, and cannibals to slash their way down a decades-long blood-splattered red carpet toward box-office gold. He celebrated each sequel with a lone ticket to a midnight showing and a large popcorn and Cherry Coke. Michael, Jason, and Freddy escorted him from the small town to the big city. Adult braces and a gym membership forged a formerly effete youth into the model Chelsea boy. He had the looks and the job but was unwilling to leave behind his adolescent obsessions. If anything, his passion matured with him.

❖

The cacophony of the multitude rose and flashes from several hundred cameras illuminated a sea of North Face jackets propping up heads pricked by cheap devil horns and cat ear headbands. Momentarily distracted from his census, Stephen followed the crowd's attention as the zombie crew of a downed airplane shambled up Sixth Avenue—stewardesses with jagged pieces of metal hanging from their stomachs lurched behind zombie pilots; one limped and clutched the controls torn from its moorings while the copilot had one arm tucked none too discreetly into his flight jacket to simulate a missing limb. A zombie passenger bore a broken propeller like Jesus laboring beneath the cross. Two dead passengers brought up the rear hauling the tail of the plane, a miracle of papier-mâché affixed to an old baby stroller. He noted that the stewardesses wore matching Pan Am uniforms and that the company logo was also painted onto the remnants of the wing bandied about by a dead passenger. He admitted that the spectacle was certainly worthy of the crowd's attention. But not his; he was busy counting Michaels.

For years Stephen had mulled over a half-formed theory that horror aficionados could be divided into the three categories of primarily Michael, Jason, or Freddy fans. Each killer represented a specific type. Freddy fans were permanent adolescents worked into a lather over Freddy's repartee in the *Nightmare on Elm Street* series more than the thrill of the kill. Pimply nerds, these were gamers and Goth kids who drifted over to horror to satisfy but a shelf on the bookcase of their D&D and heavy metal taste. Jason fans were brutish, big, and tallied kills like baseball statistics while identifying with the big guy himself more as a loner, a source of strength rather than a murder machine. To them, Jason justifiably hunted revenge in the *Friday the 13th* films. Fans of Michael Myers from *Halloween* were different. Michael was the lone introspective killer among the three. He plotted his kills with an irony that Freddy's laugh-track-ready monologue lacked. Silent like Jason, his quietude was more than predatory but a force unto itself. Not that Stephen looked down on the other two bloodied behemoths, he was just *drawn* to Michael, the one killer whose perspective the viewer shared, looking out at the world from behind a mask.

Four gay boys jogged by, each representing a member of the Fantastic Four. The twink dressed as the Invisible Woman shrieked with laughter as a seemingly straight Puerto Rican boy in a Zorro mask lunged at the bobbing balloons spilling out of his blue leotard. The boy pulled on his crotch as he returned to his laughing friends while the shirtless gym bunny painted orange to represent the Thing shot him a scornful look. Stephen knew midnight was approaching. The imperceptible strictures of society were loosened as the darkness deepened and alcohol took hold. Some masks would come off tonight, others would tighten and contort until they became the face of the wearer, and for a few hours, anything would be possible.

❖

Twelve Michaels so far. Not a good number. He decided to avoid the crowds on Christopher Street. Tons of people converged there after the parade. If he was lucky enough to score a spot by one of the metallic barriers, he'd be able to scan the crowd for more Michaels. Years ago when he first initiated the census, he had counted all three film characters, noting increases whenever a particular fiend had a movie out, though now that all three franchises had been resurrected and reworked to his distaste, he felt a certain parity had been reached. That meant whichever killer was more represented had a stronger hold on the collective unconscious. The men who dressed as

Jason tended toward large and stocky hams, playing it up for the crowd with a diminutive girlfriend in tow. The field of Freddies was typically skinny and obnoxious, always part of a group of guys dressed as other recognizable figures from pop culture. Clowns in striped sweaters were distinguishable only for the effort put into assembling the clawed gloves Freddy was so famous for. A movie memorabilia company had started pumping out affordable likenesses, however, so even that had lost its edge.

Michael remained the focal point of his interest. A gas station attendant suit, a rubber mask, and a plastic knife might sound like the easiest costume to assemble, but the philosophy of Michael Myers could be channeled by whoever donned the attire of the killer. Unique among the trinity was Michael's stance. Freddy sulked, and Jason stalked, but Michael *waited*. Stephen got a particular thrill from the Michaels who positioned themselves on a street corner or in a lonesome segment of Union Square and stood stock still. These guys had a complete commitment to the role. They understood that real fear resides not in what is coming after you, but what lies in wait.

There was an unusual uptick in Richard Simmons costumes this year, and Stephen wondered if the queeny exercise guru had died or been arrested. The throng on the side street was less boisterous than the group following the parade, and though most were costumed, they seemed on their way to parties or were high or inebriated. A tallish Pinhead from the *Hellraiser* films labored under the weight of his leather overcoat. Even though the night was chilly, the sweat on his brow threatened to upend the fake nails glued to his shaved head. Stephen could tell the man had regretted his choice of costumes and was simply soldiering on. He'd never counted Pinheads and took comfort no one had made a discernable effort to add him to the modern pantheon of horror.

Sure, the first two films were rightfully considered cult classics, and though Stephen owned special editions of each and had read all of Clive Barker's books, the *Hellraiser* films didn't have the pull of the other franchises, all of which launched earlier (*Halloween* being the first), paving the way for all others. Even if the numerous sequels to each film were of varying quality, none of the subsequent *Hellraiser* sequels possessed enough overt elements of terror or even daring splatter to matter. Interestingly enough, Stephen had read that after the success of the *Freddy vs. Jason* film, Barker and the director of *Halloween*, John Carpenter, held serious talks about a face-off between the two entities. Still, no matter how unfulfilling a latter day Michael-Jason-Freddy film might have been, whenever blade connected to flesh, the old spark was lit, adrenaline pumped.

The most Michaels he had counted during one parade were twenty-one, the year Rob Zombie released the first of his reimagined *Halloween* films. Stephen left the theater after twenty minutes, appalled at the license the untalented musician inflicted upon Michael. The added backstory inflicted too much definition on a character billed as "The Shape" in the original film's credits. He took smug satisfaction that his lowest count of Michaels came the year Rob Zombie's sequel was released. Tonight, though, he needed to get his numbers up, even if he had to stay out all night to do it. A few blocks from the pier, he saw another Michael across the street.

That makes thirteen.

And he was alone with this Michael, the streets momentarily deserted though the muffled sounds of raucous parade noise could be heard in the distance. This Michael was perfect: the right height, the mask as white as an unstained sheet, and the knife glistening slightly beneath the street lamp.

Because the knife is real.

Stephen felt his heartbeat quicken. Panic deepened within his lungs as he struggled to keep from breathing too rapidly. Michael cocked his head and regarded him from behind the impenetrable rubber of his mask. Stephen was transfixed as the figure stepped forward between two parked cars. Michael stopped and slowly unzipped his jumpsuit, revealing a sculpted chest and a stomach cradled by a surge of dark hair, though Stephen was hypnotized by the even darker tattoo of a devil's head that spread across the man's chest.

The devil's downcast skull bore elongated horns—the unseen tips wrapped around his now exposed shoulders as the jumpsuit slid farther down his torso. Each nipple was the calm center of the tattoo's malicious eyes. Stephen stared as Michael let loose a torrent of steaming piss. The urine pooled between his spread legs and began to wind across the street toward where Stephen was standing. Michael's cock was in shadow, but Stephen could tell from the way the killer handled his equipment that it was of considerable length—likely as lethal as his knife. He felt his arousal grow and realized that his mouth was open, that a speechless craving was drawing him across the street to service a man whose knife rested on the hood a parked car. An impossible amount of piss spread across the asphalt as if beckoning him forward.

The force that hit his shoulder from behind nearly knocked the wind out of him.

"Hey, man, don't *you* know it's *not* polite to *stare*?"

An eruption of laughter followed as a group of drunken boys and one delirious-looking girl in hoop earrings stumbled past. The boys all had ridiculous wolf masks pushed up past their foreheads. Their unfocused, bloodshot eyes had already moved from Stephen toward whatever mayhem awaited them at the piers. As they passed, the girl looked back at Stephen with an apologetic smirk and said, "Trick or treat, eh?"

The boys linked on either of her arms thought this was hilarious and erupted in further toothy laughter. Stephen couldn't help but think that the hollow eyes of the cartoonish wolf masks riding their skulls regarded him with further derision. He turned to face his Michael again, but the killer had zipped up the jumpsuit and stepped back onto the sidewalk. Michael picked up his knife and walked toward the pier in the same deliberate manner the Shape in the films cut through yards and hallways, the knife in his hand clutched not in anger but as extension of himself. Not a weapon but an appendage.

❖

Stephen's years in New York City had been a ladder of professional success—each year another step up. From gaining his degree in accounting to purchasing a tiny apartment off Union Square right before the neighborhood gentrified and the market exploded, he constantly moved in measured steps toward the common goals of stability and financial security. At least that was how he traveled during the light of day. His nighttime activities were far less defined and never spoken of among the company he kept. He changed jobs every three or four years, as that was the prescribed practice for anyone who wanted to freshen up a résumé, but for Stephen it was also important to change the people who surrounded him. Camaraderie at work annoyed him, and his few gay friends as well as his lone fag hag were so suitably self-absorbed that they showed little to no interest in his life. His only value to them lay in helping fill a table at brunch, that and his sharp, irrefutable financial advice at tax time.

He realized early on that his fascination with horror films was best not shared with colleagues, that his required gay friends found his interests rather déclassé. That part of him lived on the Internet, where his steady stream of pithy comments on several horror blogs made him a star in such self-contained universes, earning him invitations to go to conventions with other queers into horror, but the meetings always failed to gel. The other guys lived the life and looked the part with their piercings and dark garb. They conflicted with the image he had worked so hard to build and maintain. Stephen always upheld a professional appearance, short hair and glasses in neutral clothes from Banana Republic, the only place he shopped at, and then only when on sale.

He'd tried dating for years before he admitted to himself he was only doing it to fit in—one of the few prescriptions for being successfully gay in the city he was willing to dispense with. Before he bought his apartment, he rented a two-bedroom place in Inwood, back when it was still incredibly cheap. He was able to stock one room with his collection of movies and memorabilia. That door remained closed when dates or tricks were over. However, the move downtown to tighter quarters necessitated a decision: either get rid of or downsize his collection or be open about it to friends and visitors alike. Stephen chose neither, and further compartmentalized his life by never bringing someone home for sex or for any other reason. Ever. Every inch of wall space in his studio apartment was covered with shelves of DVDs or framed movie posters. What he needed from other men he first found within certain basement clubs in the Meat Packing District. As those subterranean vaults were absorbed by chic restaurants and postmodern hotels, he moved on to the dank video booths that populated a few of the still-seedy streets in the Garment District, a double boon for him as a Giuliani-era law required that seventy-five percent of the merchandise at such establishments consist of non-erotic material. Often, when he was finished, he was able to score the odd horror movie on the cheap.

❖

The crowd near the pier, unfettered by traffic, grew wilder. Pot smoke and dirty laughter filled the air. A flock of pasty vampires compared fangs while a bawdy gaggle of amateur drag queens were lovingly read their rights by the real things. Stephen forded the masses, Michael only a few yards ahead. He had never talked to or followed anyone dressed as Michael on Halloween before. His goal had always been to count them, assess their costume and demeanor, make mental notes and move on. But now he was pulled forward. Sheepish onlookers who hadn't bothered to dress up faded into the background as more and more people filled the sidewalk and spilled onto the street. A bacchanal-like energy slithered through the growing mob like an invisible snake.

Stephen's favorite part from any of the *Halloween* films was the opening scene of *Halloween II*. The Shape is outside, feral, roaming through the town. This extended take was shot through the eyes of his mask, so the viewer sees a world that can't tell the difference between a killer and a costume. But Stephen had never once dressed up for this holiday. He relished his role as a member of the audience. He was here to see and not be seen. To *not* dress up on this day was a form of invisibility. Tonight, though, he wanted the Michael who had revealed himself between the parked cars to see him, know him, to take him in an alley way and do the things Stephen had fantasized about—types of touch that the sticky partitions of the video booths kept from happening. Make no mistake, Stephen paid attention to the killer in the film, not the victim, but he'd always wanted to walk the divide where one becomes the other, a thin wire of blood on cold linoleum.

The man in front of him dressed as the Shape could take him there. Note that his focus was never the heroine. Only from repeated viewings did he even happen to pick up their names. This, too, set him apart from the other gay guys he met that were into these films. They tended to identify with the survivor, the strong woman who's seen it all. Stephen did not want to be the long-suffering Laurie Strode, admirably played by Jamie Lee Curtis in the first two films, reprising her role two decades later in *Halloween H2O*, which smartly ignored the preceding and mostly inconsequential sequels (though he had a soft spot for *Halloween 6: The Curse of Michael Myers*, mostly because of the actor Paul Rudd and the fact that he owned a pristine copy of the extremely rare producer's cut). He loved *H2O* and admired her character's grit and determination, but he did not relate to her trials. What he craved was to feel a measured amount of dread, to know that what was dangerous outside could never gain entry, that as an audience member he could approach this shimmering window of light again and again and coolly study the terror on the screen.

❖

A hulking Buzz Lightyear stumbled in front of him. He wove around the inebriated cartoon character, searching for his Michael when he noticed a large, well-built man dressed as the Flash walking toward him, the miniature trademark wings above his cowled ears sailing through the air. Stephen had complained in more than one chat room that the recent influx of superhero costumes had diluted the dark spirit of Halloween. Sure, there had always been Superman, Batman, and Spider-Man costumes, but the explosion of films based on comic books had flooded the costume shops with innumerable cheap Wolverines and his ilk.

But this Flash was different, and he was leering at him. Stephen went so far as to look over his shoulder to see if he was looking at someone else. As they passed one another, the throng surged, and he found himself pressed against the hard flesh of the hero. The man's green eyes burrowed into his and Stephen steadied himself by putting his palms on the Flash's chest. His eyes were the green of hidden, earthen strength, that violent growth of vine greedy to loop through the skulls of those naive enough to explore a jungle they were never meant to know. The strength of his pectorals was electrifying. More startling, frightening, was that Stephen's grip pulled the top of the masked hero's costume down, revealing the tattoo of a devil's cranium, with horns reaching back to pull on the man's shoulders. He let go as the Flash let out a wicked laugh and spun away. Revelers filled the void, yet Stephen felt alone.

Traffic slinked up and down Hudson Street. Music blared from the windows of cars or open apartment windows, but the sidewalk was less crowded as most parade goers stuck to Christopher Street or lingered near Sixth Avenue. A too-skinny-to-be-threatening Michael with a comical cardboard knife held hands with a rather elegant Bride of Frankenstein, but Stephen didn't bother to count him. He was too rattled and needed a drink. He'd never been so thirsty. Without thinking, he headed toward Caesar's. One of the oldest gay bars in the city, it was also one of the dingiest. Populated by sour fairies and smelling of mildew, it had none of the "authentic" charm of a dive and all the filth of a dilapidated business the health department hadn't closed yet.

Sure enough, on a night where most other bars were humming wall-to-wall with spandexed and masked patrons practically throwing twenties at besieged bartenders, Caesar's had managed to pull in only a modest crowd. The lights were mercifully dim. Obnoxious show tunes wheezed out of the jukebox. The floor was covered with sawdust kicked into filthy clumps by foot traffic. The customers at the bar were mostly dressed in everyday fare. One annoying queen in a massive tutu, beard dyed a rainbow of loud colors, was the only reminder that Halloween ruled outside. Stephen wedged himself between an ancient dandy and a rotund tourist in cargo pants. He caught the eye of the usually slow-on-the-draw bartender and ordered a boilermaker. Stephen over-tipped and retreated to a corner table near the bathroom. The bar smelled of mothballs and expired lust. Stephen took the shot of whiskey and chased it with a long tug on his beer. He had hoped for a moment of solitude before the trek home, but what quiet the bar afforded was broken as a large contingent of parade goers poured inside.

Someone had put money in the jukebox and replaced the shrill, emotional sounds of Broadway with the grateful sheen of soulless disco. Stephen took another sip of his beer, trying to find a modicum of stability within the mix of liquor and music. He couldn't stop thinking about the man dressed as the Flash. He couldn't have the same menacingly entrancing tattoo as Michael Myers. He finished his drink and let out a silent, sulfuric belch. He had needed to piss for a while but did not want to surrender his seat now that the bar was filling up. The more he thought about the Flash, the more he seemed less a comic book character and more like something from somewhere *else*, the wings astride his head Mercurial, pagan.

What message was he trying to deliver, though? And his eyes were too green, like jade but fired by a potent light. At once primal, filled with abandon yet demanding obedience. He never saw the eyes of the Michael who'd exposed himself between the parked cars, but maybe he wasn't supposed to. Maybe what was being communicated to him had to be whispered in stages—he was being confronted with familiar images to better prepare him for the unknown.

He closed his eyes. Michael Myers, the Shape, the cinematic killer with the real blade that he had followed, he could cut through the dividing walls between him and the countless men he serviced in the video booths. But without those walls to contain and channel his desire, what would they do to and for each other? Stephen shuddered as the images of blood and urine and cum he'd worked so hard at sublimating paraded through his mind. He was annoyed that he had finished his drink and was prevented by his now raging hard-on from going to the bar to order another. He shifted uncomfortably in his seat as a shadow fell across his table.

"I've bought you a drink."

He looked up at the figure looming before him and felt his skin turn cold. The man wore tight red leather pants pulled low to reveal a sprawl of pubic hair lapping at his rippled stomach. His upper body was crossed with studded leather straps as if attempting to restrain the now-familiar tattoo of a devil. The man's face was hidden behind a devil mask—a contoured, be-horned replica of the demonic tattoo that colored his torso. It was as if he had stepped out of the Shape's chest, spun away from under Mercury's shirt and into this bar to buy him a drink.

The masked man turned an empty chair around so its back faced the table and straddled it, holding the glass seductively close to Stephen's mouth. Stephen searched his mind for any facts concerning gifts from the Devil. Now that the man in the devil mask was closer, he could see the blond stubble on his jagged chin, little hairs lightened by hellfire. His guest smiled back at him as if in on the joke. His skin was well tanned and swarthy, as if he hadn't bathed recently. His arms were nicked and raked with scars. *Suckling demons that momentarily got the best of him?* Stephen thought, dryly. The drink shone amber and then black as the man in the devil mask rotated the glass in his nicotine-stained fingers, his nails blackened at the edges. A lifetime of thirst constricted Stephen's throat. He looked into the green eyes of the man in the devil mask and the emerald waterfalls within parted. Jade panthers cut through the veldt inside his irises and bared black fangs. Stephen had the answer to his question: *If I accept a drink from the devil, will I become his slave?*

He grabbed the proffered glass and guzzled greedily, his reply swirling around the crushed ice clanking against his teeth.

I hope so.

Stephen didn't remember entering the bathroom with the man in the devil mask. First they had shared several drinks and laughed and put dollars in the jukebox and groped one another, and the man bought a round of shots for everyone at the bar. They cheered him and hoisted their glasses as he howled and Bryan Ferry coyly crooned his version of "Sympathy for the Devil" through the blown speakers. They shared many small kisses and secrets before they ended up in the cramped commode, Stephen on his knees, dampness soaking through his jeans as he unbuckled the pants of his satanic majesty. He recoiled when he saw that the thing that tumbled out was pitch-black and slick and scaly like a snake, a serpent who commanded him to do things he didn't know he wanted to do, things he had fought hard to keep in the back of his mind when cocks slid through the slats of the video booths like mail he had to read with his tongue. When the man in the devil mask pissed on his face, he eagerly drank every drop even though it tasted like blood.

Any man who entered the bathroom at Caesar's that night fell under the erotic fugue of the tiny space, and Stephen serviced them all. They cracked him open like a book and studied his every orifice, tested his every previously untapped talent, returning only if the man in the devil mask ordered them to do so, often delivering a drink in one hand, pushing a surprised friend into the bathroom with the other. At some point, Stephen lost his glasses. The shadowy image of the man in the devil mask sometimes blurred into that of the Flash. One time Stephen looked up to see what he thought was Michael Myers wearing a pink feathered boa and holding a martini. When the bartender came to investigate, he was immediately enlisted. As his eyes rolled toward the back of his head, he gripped Stephen by the ears and fucked his face, stopping occasionally to utter crude phrases in Latin.

It was anticlimactic when, near dawn, the man in the devil mask finally removed his disguise and revealed a face that was exactly as his mask had been: a hard red skin, bony and resilient. The horns that rolled from out the top of his head even expanded a bit, as if the pretense of the mask had somehow bridled their length and power. The demon lit a cigarette retrieved from the pants pocket of a passed-out clown, a poor drunken figure who'd entered the bathroom an hour ago to relieve himself and instead sodomized Stephen several times over, eyes closed, red rubber nose half off his face, tears of frustration ruining his white makeup. Stephen felt as if he were a pancake flipped too many times, singed and without form, but he answered the renewed call of his master, and as the hellion smoked a stale Pall Mall, Stephen again swallowed the obsidian cock placed in his mouth. It tasted like burnt leather. He was mildly intrigued to notice that as the scaly penis engorged within his throat, he could feel a hundred or so tiny demonic eyes flutter open, affording the Devil a view from the inside. For Stephen, the miniscule eyelashes tickled and made him giggle before he gagged on the molten semen that would provide a fitting and noxious sealant to his fate.

❖

An anchorman blathered about the weather on the television in the next room. Stephen whistled as he showered. His throat was sore from the previous night, so after brushing his teeth and gargling with Listerine, he ran down to the Duane Reade that consumed the entire ground floor of his building. He bought some Halls cough drops, choosing a new dark cherry flavor. Though he'd not gotten a minute of sleep, he felt spry and ready. He also picked up a cheap plastic devil mask, already marked down by fifty percent. He paid for it and the cough drops and donned the mask before leaving the pharmacy.

Stephen decided to walk to work. He had put on his Brooks Brothers suit, his favorite, purchased at considerable discount at the Century 21 Department Store years ago. He'd rarely had the occasion to wear it. He'd skipped wearing an overcoat, as it wasn't that cold and a brisk walk would keep him from feeling a chill. He hardly got any strange looks as he walked up Broadway. The sidewalk was littered with crushed plastic cups, strips of police tape, glitter, and vomit. The cloudless sky was a mix of bleary blue and newborn pink, the jumble of office buildings gray and empty. The elastic band of the mask dug into the back of his head. Sure, it was inevitable that someone would say something about his crimson disguise once the office filled up, but he wasn't worried. His briefcase swung jauntily by his side. It held a few pieces of nondescript mail and a large kitchen knife. That was the only answer he needed.

ABOUT THE AUTHOR

Tom Cardamone is the author of the Lambda Literary Award–winning speculative novella *Green Thumb* and the erotic fantasy novel *The Werewolves of Central Park* as well as the novella *Pacific Rimming*. His short story collection, *Pumpkin Teeth*, was a finalist for the Lambda Literary Award and Black Quill Award. Additionally, he has edited *The Lost Library: Gay Fiction Rediscovered* and the anthology *Lavender Menace: Tales of Queer Villainy!*, which was nominated for the Over The Rainbow List by the LGBT Round Table of the American Library Association. His short stories have appeared in numerous anthologies and magazines, some of which have been collected on his website: www.pumpkinteeth.net.

Books Available From Bold Strokes Books

Night Sweats by Tom Cardamone. These stories are as gripping as the hand on your throat. (978-1-62639-572-5)

Soul's Blood by Stephen Graham King. After receiving a summons from a love long past, Keene and his associates, Lexa-Blue and the sentient ship Maverick Heart, are plunged into turmoil on a planet poised for war. (978-1-62639-508-4)

Corpus Calvin by David Swatling. Cloverkist Inn may be haunted, but a ghost materializes from Jason Dekker's past and Calvin's canine instinct kicks in to protect a young boy from mortal danger. (978-1-62639-428-5)

Brothers by Ralph Josiah Bardsley. Blood is thicker than water, but you can drown in either. Jamus Cork and Sean Malloy struggle against tradition to find love in the Irish enclave of South Boston. (978-1-62639-538-1)

Every Unworthy Thing by Jon Wilson. Gang wars, racial tensions, a kidnapped girl, and a lone PI! What could go wrong? (978-1-62639-514-5)

Puppet Boy by Christian Baines. Budding filmmaker Eric can't stop thinking about the handsome young actor that's transferred to his class. Could Julien be his muse? Even his first boyfriend? Or something far more sinister? (978-1-62639-510-7)

The Prophecy by Jerry Rabushka. Religion and revolution threaten to bring an ancient civilization to its knees...unless love does it first. (978-1-62639-440-7)

Heart of the Liliko'i by Dena Hankins. Secrets, sabotage, and grisly human remains stall construction on an ancient Hawaiian burial ground, but the sexual connection between Kerala and Ravi keeps building toward a volcanic explosion. (978-1-62639-556-5)

Lethal Elements by Joel Gomez-Dossi. When geologist Tom Burrell is hired to perform mineral studies in the Adirondack Mountains, he finds himself lost in the wilderness and being chased by a hired gun. (978-1-62639-368-4)

The Heart's Eternal Desire by David Holly. Sinister conspiracies threaten Seaton French and his lover, Dusty Marley, and only by tracking the source of the conspiracy can Seaton and Dusty hold true to the heart's eternal desire. (978-1-62639-412-4)

The Orion Mask by Greg Herren. After his father's death, Heath comes to Louisiana to meet his mother's family and learn the truth about her death—but some secrets can prove deadly. (978-1-62639-355-4)

The Strange Case of the Big Sur Benefactor by Jess Faraday. Billiwack, CA, 1884. All Rosetta Stein wanted to do was test her new invention. Now she has a mystery, a stalker, and worst of all, a partner. (978-1-62639-516-9)

One Hot Summer Month by Donald Webb. Damien, an avid cockhound, flits from one sexual encounter to the next until he finally meets someone who assuages his sexual libido. (978-1-62639-409-4)

The Indivisible Heart by Patrick Roscoe. An investigation into a gruesome psycho-sexual murder and an account of the victim's final days are interwoven in this dark detective story of the human heart. (978-1-62639-341-7)

Fool's Gold by Jess Faraday. 1895. Overworked secretary Ira Adler thinks a trip to America will be relaxing. But rattlesnakes, train robbers, and the U.S. Marshals Service have other ideas. (978-1-62639-340-0)

Big Hair and a Little Honey by Russ Gregory. Boyfriend troubles abound as Willa and Grandmother land new ones and Greg tries to hold on to Matt while chasing down a shipment of stolen hair extensions. (978-1-62639-331-8)

Death by Sin by Lyle Blake Smythers. Two supernatural private detectives in Washington, D.C., battle a psychotic supervillain spreading a new sex drug that only works on gay men, increasing the male orgasm and killing them. (978-1-62639-332-5)

Buddha's Bad Boys by Alan Chin. Six stories, six gay men trudging down the road to enlightenment. What they each find is the last thing in the world they expected. (978-1-62639-244-1)

Play It Forward by Frederick Smith. When the worlds of a community activist and a pro basketball player collide, little do they know that their dirty little secrets can lead to a public scandal...and an unexpected love affair. (978-1-62639-235-9)

GingerDead Man by Logan Zachary. Paavo Wolfe sells horror but isn't prepared for what he finds in the oven or the bathhouse; he's in hot water again, and the killer is turning up the heat. (978-1-62639-236-6)

Myth and Magic: Queer Fairy Tales, edited by Radclyffe and Stacia Seaman. Myth, magic, and monsters—the stuff of childhood dreams (or nightmares) and adult fantasies. (978-1-62639-225-0)

Balls & Chain by Eric Andrews-Katz. In protest of the marriage equality bill, the son of Florida's governor has been kidnapped. Agent Buck 98 is back, and the alligators aren't the only things biting. (978-1-62639-218-2)

Blackthorn by Simon Hawk. Rian Blackthorn, Master of the Hall of Swords, vowed he would not give in to the advances of Prince Corin, but he finds himself dueling with more than swords as Corin pursues him with determined passion. (978-1-62639-226-7)

Café Eisenhower by Richard Natale. A grieving young man who travels to Eastern Europe to claim an inheritance finds friendship, romance, and betrayal, as well as a moving document relating a secret lifelong love affair. (978-1-62639-217-5)

Murder in the Arts District by Greg Herren. An investigation into a new and possibly shady art gallery in New Orleans' fabled Arts District soon leads Chanse into a dangerous world of forgery, theft…and murder. A Chanse MacLeod mystery. (978-1-62639-206-9)

Calvin's Head by David Swatling. Jason Dekker and his dog, Calvin, are homeless in Amsterdam when they stumble on the victim of a grisly murder—and become targets for the calculating killer, Gadget. (978-1-62639-193-2)

The Return of Jake Slater by Zavo. Jake Slater mistakenly believes his lover, Ben Masters, is dead. Now a wanted man in Abilene, Jake rides to Mexico to begin a new life and heal his broken heart. (978-1-62639-194-9)

Rise of the Thing Down Below by Daniel W. Kelly. Nothing kills sex on the beach like a fishman out of water… Third in the Comfort Cove Series. (978-1-62639-207-6)

First Exposure by Alan Chin. Navy Petty Officer Skyler Thompson battles homophobia from his shipmates, the military, and his wife when he takes a second job at a gay-owned florist. Rather than yield to pressure to quit, he battles homophobia in order to nurture his artistic talents. (978-1-62639-082-9)

The Fall of the Gay King by Simon Hawk. Investigative journalist Logan Walker receives a mysterious erotic journal that details the sexual relations of a corporate giant known in the business world as the "Gay King of Kings." (978-1-62639-076-8)

Backstrokes by Dylan Madrid. When pianist Crawford Paul meets lifeguard Armando Leon, he accepts Armando's offer to help him overcome his fear of water by way of private lessons. As friendship turns into a summer affair, their lust for one another turns to love. (978-1-62639-069-0)

The Raptures of Time by David Holly. Mack Frost and his friends journey across an alien realm, through homoerotic adventures, suffering humiliation and rapture, making friends and enemies, always seeking a gateway back home to Oregon. (978-1-62639-068-3)

CPSIA information can be obtained
at www.ICGtesting.com
Printed in the USA
BVOW06s2142070218
507584BV00001B/9/P

9 781626 395725